ILLUSTRATIONS

SHORT STORIES BY
LEE BROWN

Epigraph Books
Rhinebeck, New York

Book and front cover design; cover art: Amy Manso
Photo of cover art: Ian Wickstead

ISBN: 978-1-966293-08-8

Library of Congress Control number: 2025906635
Epigraph Books
22 East Market Street, Suite 304
Rhinebeck, NY 12572
845.876.4861

FOR RAINN & BLAIZE

*This small collection of stories is dedicated to all the people
who will stand up to the threat of fascism so that
their children and grandchildren will not have to.*

ILLUSTRATIONS

The enclosed stories follow common citizens, superheroes and assassins trying to manage events in their daily lives; characters trying to make sense of their world.

The collection also includes a noir quiz of sorts.

Morning Porch Blues

John opened his door and stepped out onto his back porch. The sun had just made it over the treetops across the field and the morning chill was burning off.

John sat down on his favorite chair and took a satisfied sip of his coffee. He put his coffee cup on the floor and smiled at the cover of his new book: "All Shot Up" by Chester Himes. This was a great book, he thought, and he was determined to finish it that morning. He opened the book to page 57. He read one sentence that he had read the day before when the tip of a shoe beyond the porch railing caught his attention. He laid the book in his lap and put his palms flat over the open pages. He frowned and then leaned forward. Through the rails of the porch more of a green canvas shoe appeared. It was a little disturbing to John because the shoe's tip pointed straight to the sky.

John leaned back. He looked to his left and then swiveled his head to the right. He looked at the shoe tip again. Leaning to his left he laid his book down on the floor opposite from his coffee. When he straightened up, he pursed his lips and began to slowly rise from his seat. He paused with both hands holding the arms of his chair. He could see something was attached to

■ ● ■

the shoe. A leg. He looked to the left and right again, somehow feeling guilty. He took a deep breath, and stepped forward. As he did he looked over his shoulder, half expecting someone to be there. But he was alone in the house.

John barely glanced over the rail. He could see that the leg was connected to a body. He took a quick step back from the railing. He rubbed his hands on the sides of his jeans, then guickly glanced left and right again. He squinted his eyes, took another deep breath, let it out slowly and stepped forward.

Lying on the ground, on his back, with one shoe pointing toward the sky, was a man in green khakis with his brown jacket open, wearing a light black sweater.

"Hey, you! You can't be slee..." John looked left and right and slid his feet to the right hoping to see the man's face better. John had been hoping to wake the man up, but his face let John know there was going to be no waking this man. In his mind he could hear Humphrey Bogart say, "He was sleeping the big sleep."

"Shi-it! And he's a white man! What the hell is a white man doing lying dead out in my back yard?! Why couldn't he be dead over at Houston's?!"

John snapped his head to the left hoping Houston hadn't heard his almost whispered laments. He looked down at the man while squeezing the railing with both hands. The man's eyes were wide open, his mouth was open about an inch.

John stood up, put both palms to his own eyes and rubbed them. He shook his head, rubbed his eyes again and went into his house.He looked around his kitchen, then walked to his telephone. He picked up the receiver, sighed and dialed for his next door neighbor, Darnell. The phone rang seven times before John heard a raspy voice.

"This had better be good seein' as its only 6:15 in the a.m."

■ ● ■

"Darnell, this is John."

"John? John who?!"

"Your next door neighbor John."

"Why in the color of hell are you calling me at 6:15, no, 6:16 in the morning?!"

"Darnell, there's a dead man lying out in my back yard."

"Really?" There was silence. "John! You playin?!"

"Darnell, go look out your kitchen window."

"Hell…I ain't got to look out any window. Call the police if you got a dead man layin' out there."

"Please, Darnell. Just take a look."

It got quiet and then John heard the bed covers move.

"God Damn, John! Hold on!" John could hear Darnell place the receiver on the night table next to his bed. He could faintly hear Darnell's feet slap the floor as he walked away from the phone. Then he heard Darnell yell, "Oh fuck! Youn't say it was a white man! Now John could hear Darnell coming back to the phone quickly. Darnell picked up the phone. "You kill that white man, John?"

"What?!"

"You kill 'em?"

"No I didn't kill him. He was dead when I went out on my porch with my coffee and my book."

"If you ain't kill 'em, who did?"

"I have no idea! I don't even know if anyone killed him. He might have had a heart attack."

Darnell responded as if he was talking to a child. "John… why would a white man be out in your backyard having a heart attack?"

John was taken aback. "Darnell…I…look, I just want to have someone else here when I called the police and they come over here."

■ ● ■

"Call the police?! Don't you call the police. Are you crazy?! You got a dead white man layin' in your little piece of lawn. The police might come in there and shoot you and me too. Hell, I ain't gettin' involved in any mess like that. Too bad he ain't dead over in Houston's back yard. Houston just dig a pit, drop that white man in it, cover him over and go down to the Garden Shop and buy some flowers to plant on top. You want, maybe I help you drag him over to Houston's."

"Nobody is dragging nobody anywhere. Forget I called, Darnell."

"How am I gonna forget that. It's twenty-five minutes after six in the mornin' and my neighbor has a dead white man, that I can see from my kitchen window, layin' out in his own backyard. And John, don't you ever wake me up this early to look at a dead man again."

While Darnell was starting another sentence, that John didn't want to hear, he hung up the phone. He moved back into his kitchen. He was staring at his stove when he heard the truck pull up next door. He sped to his living room window and pulled the shade aside. John felt relieved. Houston was home early from his job over at the college.

John moved quickly to his front door. He wanted to talk to Houston before he went into his house. John was worried that Houston might just fall asleep immediately once he stepped through his front door after working all night. John yelled Houston's name from his front porch while Houston was opening the passenger side door to his pick-up truck. Houston turned his head, raised one arm in greeting and said, "John."

John rushed over to Houston's truck at a speed which caught Houston by surprise. Pulling back from John, and with a frown on his face, Houston said, "How you doin' this mornin', John?"

"Not so great."

■ ● ■

"Sorry to hear that. Rheumatism?"

John looked at Houston confused. "Rheumatism? I've never had Rheumatism."

"I thought you told me once you had the Rheumatism." Houston turned away, looking relieved that John didn't have Rheumatism. He started gathering his things from the passenger's seat.

John was still confused. "Houston, I need you to take a look at something."

"Oh yeah?"

"Yeah. Like right now."

"You want me to look at something right now? I've been working all night, John. What is it?"

John looked around hoping there was no one to hear him. In a whisper he said, "It's out in my back yard."

Houston sighed, put his things back on the seat and closed the truck door. He thought John was acting a little odd. "Okay, let's go."

John and Houston started walking down the alley that separated their homes. Houston always made John feel small, even though he wasn't. John and Houston were the same height, but Houston was stocky. John sometimes thought of Houston as four feet wide from feet to neck. In the alley way Houston's large size seemed to be confirmed.

When they got to the corners of their respective homes they stopped.

"Why are you letting somebody sleep out in your backyard? We don't need this kind of thing going on about here. Why didn't you just chase him off, John. Damn, I'll do it right now if you're not!"

"He's not sleeping."

Houston frowned at John. Then just tell the son of a bitch to

■ ● ■

be on his way. He's got no business back here. You don't know him, do you?"

John shook his head.

"Well then…" Houston walked toward the man on the ground in a purposeful stride, then slowed. "If he ain't sleepin', is he knocked out?" He looked down at the man and slid sideways, moving his left foot and then his right to catch up with the left. Houston stopped, folded his arms across his chest, tilted his head and said, "Motherfucker dead." Houston straightened his head and stared at John. "When you kill this motherfucker, John?"

John's head snapped back like he had been punched.

"I didn't kill anybody!"

"Then what's he doin' in your backyard, next to your back porch?"

John was exasperated. "I don't know how he got here. I don't know if someone killed him…"

"Course someone killed him. He's dead."

"Maybe he had a heart attack."

Houston looked at John like he didn't understand. "Why would a man…why would a white man walk into your backyard to have a heart attack?" Houston looked down at the body. "Want me to close his eyes?"

"Don't touch anything, Houston."

Houston walked back over to John, who was still standing at the corner of his house. Houston stood about one foot from John and looked over his shoulder at the corpse. In a conspiratorial whisper Houston said, "Look, man. Let me get some sleep. When its dark I'll help you drag him out to the curb."

A high pitched, James Brown inspired, "What?!" exploded from John's lips.

"Well I didn't mean we'd just leave him out front of your

■ ● ■

house. We can drag him on down the street somewhere."

John looked at Huston incredulously. "We're not dragging any dead body anywhere!"

"Then what are you gonna' do?"

"Call the police."

Houston looked directly into John's eyes and took a step back. He tilted his head and began to smile. Then he grinned and finally bent over in laughter.

"What the hell is so funny?"

Houston tried to straighten up and then bent over again. Houston finally stood up straight no longer laughing. He wiped the tears from his eyes and chuckled. "I'm sorry, John. I need some sleep." A faint smile left Houston's face.

"You're serious."

"Yeah, I'm serious and I was hoping you could be witness as to what happens when the police get here."

"That's a white man layin' over there. How much trouble you lookin' to have today?"

John just looked at Houston. Houston started to feel uncomfortable. John's stare was becoming unnerving.

Houston turned back toward the corpse. "Okay, John. I'll be out here if you call the cops to come over here." Houston turned back to John and whispered, "Look, man, I won't say anything to anyone. But if you killed that motherfucker I think you should let me know before anything crazy breaks off."

John shook his head and rolled his eyes. "Houston, I didn't kill that man. I don't know how he died. Did you see any marks on his body?"

Houston's eyebrows raised. "You right. I didn't see any blood whatsoever." Houston folded his arms. "Maybe somebody strangled him or poisoned him."

"Yeah, uh-huh…look, Houston…I'm going to put in that call.

■●■

Can I come get you when the cops get here?"

"Sure, man. I'll be nappin' on my couch. I'll leave the front door unlocked. Just come and get me."

John watched Houston walk down the alley. He looked at the body laying in the grass and then went inside to call the police department.

When he picked up the phone he saw Reverend Taylor out on the sidewalk talking to Darnell, who was still in his pajamas. John put the phone down and walked to his living room window. Suddenly Darnell and Reverend Taylor both waved down the street. John pulled the shade to the side. They were waving to Houston, who was climbing the stairs to his house, and apparently to Attie-Mae Kendricks, who was walking up the sidewalk.

John returned to the phone and dialed the police department. He told a desk sergeant that there was a body in his backyard. He gave his name and phone number. When he gave his address and asked how soon he could expect someone, the sergeant said, "Yep," and hung up.

John went out to his front porch to wait for the police. An hour later John was still waiting. John decided to go back in his house and clean his breakfast dishes. As he got close to the kitchen John thought he heard music. He stepped toward his radio to turn it off but it wasn't playing. John looked around his living room, then realized it was a hymn. It couldn't be Darnell. He never played spiritual music. He was more in tune with T-Bone Walker. Houston had to be asleep by then and he never heard music come from Houston's house. It was coming from his kitchen.

John walked into the kitchen and then felt foolish. The music was coming from outside. John thought it must be the Baptists. But then it struck him that it was Thursday morning.

■ ● ■

Why would the Baptists be in church on a Thursday morning, at this hour?

John looked out through the screen door. It slammed against the wall of his house when he pushed it open in anger.

Reverend Taylor was reading scripture from Psalms. Three women were humming a spiritual as he read from his bible. The women swayed back and forth in time with the tune. One of them was slightly off-key.

"What the hell are y'all doing out here?! That's a dead man! Go on home Attie-Mae. You too, Virginia."

"We are reading from the Good Book this…"

"Not in my backyard you're not. I thought you'd have more sense, Althea. Go on! Go on home!"

"You can't raise your voice and talk to us like that!"

"You don't live here no more, Althea. You can let your legs carry you on down the road, too."

Attie-Mae and Virginia were moving reluctantly away from the body. John was getting frustrated watching them.

"Police will be here soon. Just letting you know."

At that the Reverend Taylor slapped his bible closed and quickly disappeared left down John's driveway. The two women broke into a quick-step to the right, going through the alley way. Althea stood over the body with her hands on her hips, with her pink pocketbook dangling from her right hand.

"You can't talk to us like that."

John waved his hand at her. "You still don't have a lick of sense." He grabbed the screen door and closed it as he went back into the kitchen. He grabbed a dish rag while listening to Althea's footsteps climb the stairs to his porch. The screen door opened and closed without John turning around.

"Next time knock before you come in."

"I will never knock to come in here."

■ ● ■

"You better learn. You don't live here anymore, Althea."

"I can't come in my own house?!"

John turned around. "You really must be out of your mind. This is not your house anymore. Hasn't been your house for two years. We are divorced. You got money. I got the house. Donald still have his house?"

"I hope you burn. I never ever want to hear about Donald again."

"Then don't come in my kitchen."

Althea looked at John with the daggers of Leviticus streaming from her eyes." I knew it would come to this. I knew eventually you would cross the Lord and kill someone. You just got it in you. And a white man at that!"

"That's why were divorced, Althea. Anything bad happened, it must have been my fault. Anything good, praise the Lord for showing the way. A man is dead on my property and I must have had a hand in it."

"You're Godless. You certainly must have had a hand in it. If you didn't do it, you must have condoned it."

"Althea…shut up and get out of my house. What I ever saw in you is a mystery to me still."

"The mystery is how that white man came to be dead in our backyard."

John stood perfectly still until a smile flickered across his face. "You know, I haven't seen you in four or five weeks. When I do it's the same day as a dead man shows up in 'our' backyard. That, is the second thing I will have to tell the police when they get here."

"What's the first, atheist?"

"Your address."

"What?"

"Uh-huh…police might want to question you."

■ ● ■

Althea's eyes narrowed. "You're no good. You just evil." She turned and slammed the screen door open as she strode out. John walked over to the door and pulled the screen quietly shut. John started talking to himself. "What did I ever see in that woman? Her mother. Her mother convinced me to marry her. I liked her mother more than Althea. I guess I thought Althea would eventually turn into her mother. I should have married Althea's mother if I was smart. Well that didn't happen, did it, fool. And why am I talking out loud to myself like this?" John shrugged his shoulders like he couldn't explain anything to anyone.

He walked back over to the sink and glanced at the calendar next to the refrigerator. 'Three and a half years since we were married. The best day of that marriage was the day she told me that the Lord had led her to Donald.' John paused and looked around his kitchen. 'At least I'm not talking to myself right out loud.'

John picked up his dish rag just as Houston came out of his back door with a blanket over something long. He laid the blanket down at the edge of his back porch.

John dropped the dish rag and wiped his hands on his pants when he realized Houston was coming over to his house. John went to the screen door. As Houston climbed the stairs to the porch he said, "Police ain't here yet?"

"They probably think if someone is dead, there ain't no hurry. He's not going anywhere anyway."

"You tell them he's white?"

"No. I didn't want them to get cranked up before they got here."

Houston frowned. "That's a good point, but they'd probably already been here if they knew he was white."

"What do you have under that blanket over on your porch?"

■ ● ■

"Insurance. You got any coffee made up, John?"

"Insurance?" John couldn't take his eyes off the blanket. "Yeah, coffee's hot on the stove." John suddenly realized what Houston had under the blanket. "Houston! You put your twelve gauge under that blanket?"

"Yes, sir. If some peckerwood policeman decides he needs to shoot someone to solve the crime, I'm not going to be convicted by his thirty-eight."

John turned around to face Houston. "Have you lost your mind? You are preparing to shoot it out with the police force over a crime that you did not commit? There may not have even been a crime committed, Houston. What sense does it make to have your twelve gauge out on the back porch?"

"The sense that some white cracker policemen are going to come back here in our community with loaded guns and we should expect them to act right?! In fifty years white policemen will still be shooting at us and if we take some of them with us, maybe in fifty years they won't be shootin' so many of us. That's what sense it makes."

John started to open his mouth, but words wouldn't come out. A good part of what Houston said made sense abstractly. But not in this case, thought John. Or did it?

"I'm going back out on the front porch to wait."

"You make a good cup of coffee, John. Anybody ever tell you that?"

"Yeah. Althea's mother."

"I'm gonna drink this on my back porch. Maybe read the paper."

John went out to his front porch wondering why things had to be so crazy the second day of his vacation. He sat for five minutes wondering if he should try to read his book and finally decided he wouldn't be able to concentrate on it. He

■ ● ■

heard a scraping noise and some cans bang together back in the driveway. He stood up to go see what it was when he saw a black Chevy coming slowly down the street. It had to be police. He was surprised it wasn't a cruiser.

John hesitantly walked out to the sidewalk and half waved to the car. It stopped right in front of John's house. The window rolled down and a detective with a crew cut said, "Mornin'." John nodded.

"You the one with the body in his backyard?" John nodded again. The crew cut frowned.

"Yes, sir." John felt his lips tighten like he was resigning himself to a day full of trouble.

The detectives got out of the car and followed John down the driveway. At the corner of the back porch John came up short. The two detectives walked past him. The driver disinterestedly asked, "So where's the body?"

John felt dizzy. "It was right here. Right here since early this morning."

The cop with the crew cut noticed Houston sitting on his back porch drinking coffee.

" 'Scuse me. Did you see a man out here in the grass this morning?" The detective turned to John. "It was a man, right?"

John nodded and looked toward Houston.

"Yes, sir, I did. I thought he was dead. I saw John, there, shake him with his foot a few times with no response. Then he was gone when I came out with my coffee. Didn't the ambulance or coroner take him away?"

The cop who had driven said, "An ambulance was here?"

"I don't know. Just sayin' that's what I thought. He's gone now though, ain't he?"

The crew cut cop said to John, "You think maybe you couldn't tell he was just passed out drunk and he got up and walked

■ ● ■

away?"

John swallowed hard. From Houston's porch he heard, "Could'a happened that way." John stared at Houston and without looking at the detectives said, "I'm truly sorry. After I..."

The scream from Darnell's house was so blood curdling, the detective who drove pulled his gun from his holster. Everyone was looking at Darnell's house. Seconds later Darnell flew out his back door and turned to go at John, until he saw the two policemen, one of whom had a pistol in his hand.

The crew cut detective frowned and said, "Boy, you all right?"

Darnell looked confused standing there in his pajamas. His eyes went from one detective to John, to the other detective, to the pistol.

"Rats."

"The what you say?!" The crew cut cop had a deeper frown. The driver started laughing.

"We don't deal with rats. You got to get some arsenic and some cat food." He put his gun back in his holster while still laughing.

John turned his head to look at Houston. He was pulling his hand from under the blanket and beginning to stand up.

"Collins, let's get out of here. You know, you people need to learn the difference between a man who is breathing and one who's not."

John watched the two policemen walk down the driveway. Darnell moved back toward his house, glaring at John and muttering in a threatening tone, "I'll be back. Let me get me some clothes on and I'll be back."

John noticed Houston standing at his shoulder.

"Here's your coffee cup, John."

Without looking at him, "Where's that body, Houston?"

"Huh?"

■ ● ■

"I said, where is that body?" John turned to look at Houston's face.

"In Darnell's house."

"And how did it get there? Like I gotta' ask."

"I slid it in through that basement window." He pointed to a basement window that was slightly ajar. "We had to do somethin'. You saw how fast that cracker pulled his piece."

"We?! We didn't have to do anything but let those two policemen get that body out of my backyard!"

"Well it's gone now."

"Gone? Darnell looked like he was interested in homicide when he came out of that kitchen door."

"Well, then it's a good thing those two cops were here."

John looked at his shoes and thought, 'Is there some place I can go? Is there some place I can hide?'

The back door to Darnell's house slammed shut. John looked up and saw Darnell coming off his back porch with a knife in his right hand.

"With a knife?! Okay! Uh-huh! Come on over here, then." John started walking toward Darnell.

"Whoa, John. Slow down."

"What you think you gonna do with that knife, Darnell?"

Houston stepped in front of John.

"You put a dead white man in my house! What you think I'ma do with this knife? We gonna have a dead man in your house, too!"

"Hold on, Darnell. John didn't do that. Aren't you John's friend? We got to help him in this situation. You want to help him don't you?"

"Hell no! What kinda friend call you up at dawn and say 'come on over to my house, I got dead people you can look at with me at breakfast time? What kinda friend drops a dead white man on my work bench that I got nothin' to do with and gets paint all over my floor down there? Help? I want some help gettin' that dead man out my house!"

"Yeah. Yeah. I know. I got a plan."

"What kinda plan? Only plan I'm concerned with is getting that man out of my house. Then I'll settle up with John."

John tried to step around Houston.

"Darnell, John didn't drop that man down in your basement. I did."

Darnell's face took on the characteristics of a prune. "Why in fuck did you do that for?"

"Because John was heading for a peckerwood bushel of trouble. We have to help him out." Darnell stared at Houston with his mouth open. "Darnell, look here…I will get my truck. We will put him in the back and take him somewhere in the city and leave him off and let some other fool worry about him."

Darnell put his hands on his hips and twisted his head. "And what if y'all get caught? Don't be callin' me for no bail."

"Ain't nobody gonna get caught. Besides, you gonna be right with us. I got it all worked out. We'll be done with this and back home by nine o'clock."

"Next to y'all?! While you out drivin' that white man around, I will be sittin' in my living room watching Liberace on the television."

"We are gonna' have your help or you can carry that dead man out of your house by yourself."

"That's blackmail!"

"Uh-uh. That's friends helping a friend in a crisis. You are gonna meet us here at eight o'clock."

Houston turned to John and saw that John was still furious. "Calm down, John. We'll get this all cleaned up. We just couldn't have those cops arrest you for murder."

■ ● ■

John yanked his arm away from Houston's grip, which surprised John in that he was able to do it. Houston looked surprised in that John actually did it.

"Darnell comes at me with a knife again he'll be getting a tag on his toe!"

Houston's eyebrows raised when he saw so much rage pouring off of John. Houston put both of his hands up.

"Calm down, brother. Darnell usually means well. He's probably upset that all that paint on his work bench got knocked on the floor."

John stared at Houston. "Y'all gone as crazy as Althea. You related?"

"Stop right there. Don't get nasty. I told you not to marry that woman."

John's expression changed immediately. He put one hand to his forehead and looked around his yard. "You're right, Houston. You did warn me. But if Darnell comes at me with a knife…"

"Look here, let's rest up before we take that man downtown."

"Downtown? John looked at Houston in shock. "Why do you keep saying 'downtown'? I thought we'd be taking him somewhere secluded."

"It's a Thursday night. Couldn't be more secluded if we were out in the woods. I got to catch some sleep. I'll see you at eight."

At eight o'clock John heard Houston's truck pull into the driveway. John went outside and saw Darnell standing by his porch looking at the basement window that allowed a dead man to slip into his home. Houston got out of his truck, hitched his pants up with his thumbs, quietly said, "Let's get this over with. I have to go to work later."

Darnell came away from his back porch to stand next to the driveway.

■ ● ■

John was still feeling angry. "Why don't you just call in sick, or tell your boss you have to take a dead man downtown and you're gonna be a little late?"

Houston ignored John's comment and said, "You and Darnell go down in the basement and lift him up to the window. I'll pull him out and put him in the back of the truck."

"I don't want him in my house."

Houston looked at John and then at Darnell. John turned and walked past Darnell.

"Where the hell you think you goin'?" John didn't stop.

"Darnell, you think you can lift him by yourself? John didn't put that man in your house. I did. You know the police are all about taking somebody downtown. We had to do somethin'."

"Why'nt you drop him in your own basement, Houston?"

"Because all my windows are locked shut. Now get downstairs and help John get that man up to the window."

"Don't be tellin' me what to do! You ain't no master. You ain't nobody's boss. You ain't no…"

"Darnell! Just get the fuck downstairs so we can be rid of that dead motherfucker! Okay? Please, God Damn it."

Darnell slunk into his house. A few moments later an arm worked its way through the window. Houston grabbed the arm and pulled. The top of the dead man's head appeared.

"You still playin' with that dead white man?"

Houston lost his breath, his grip on the corpse, fell to one knee with his left hand pressing against the house so he wouldn't fall over. The head and arm slid back through the window and cans could be heard crashing in the basement.

"Oh God a' Mercy. Virginia, you just about stole the life out of me. What the hell are you doing here? And what are you lookin' at?"

Virginia was bent over at the waist trying to see down into

■ ● ■

Darnell's basement. She stood up and said, "Don't you start cussin' at me, Houston. I see what y'all doing in there."

The basement window opened and John's face appeared. "Houston! Why'd you let go of the man? You almost killed us. Knocked both of us off Darnell's work bench."

"Hooo! Let me catch my breath. Virginia, over here, almost give me a damn heart attack."

"Virginia?! What the hell is…"

Virginia leaned over and was face to face with John. "I see what y'all doin' here. Y'all still messin' round with that dead man. Why don't you let him go to his peace?"

From behind John, Darnell could be heard talking loud.

"John. Who you talkin' to?"

"Virginia."

"Virginia? Virginia who?"

"Virginia Kincaid. How many Virginia's do you know?"

With a sing-song voice Virginia said, "I think I should call the police."

"What she say?!"

"Quiet, Darnell. Just wait there a second, Virginia."

The window closed and then reopened. An arm slipped through. Then another arm. Houston grabbed an arm and reached for the other one.

John yelled, "Houston, just hold that one arm so he doesn't fall in here again. Virginia, grab the other arm when it comes through the window so Houston can pull him all the way out."

"What you say?! I ain't grabbin' no dead white man's arm."

"Do what he say, Virginia. We have got to get this man out of Darnell's house or he will go to prison for sure."

Virginia looked around and put her purse on the ground. She grabbed the sleeve of the man's jacket.

Houston implored her, "Pull, Virginia."

■ ● ■

The body slid through the window. Houston lifted him to his shoulder, turned and dropped him in the back of his pick up.

Virginia looked at Houston wide-eyed while he climbed into the back of his truck. "I don't think you needed my help, Houston. I think you strong enough to have done this all by yourself."

Darnell and John came around the corner of the house, quickly approaching the truck. Virginia looked at both of them. "I think I should call the police over here."

John laughed. Then Houston laughed.

"What's so funny?"

Houston climbed down out of the truck. "You an accessory, too, Virginia. You an accomplice."

Virginia's look of self-righteous determination melted away. "I ain't nothin' of the sort."

John was still laughing. "You got nosey. Then you got felonious. The excitement of something bad. Three men saw you help them hide a body. You're in this up to your purple ear rings, Virginia."

Virginia's hand raised up to fondle her naked ear lobes. "I tried to do you all a good turn. Althea is right! You are the devil's people." She turned and almost ran down the driveway. The men watched her disappear into the darkness.

"Let's go. I have to be at work in a few hours."

John stared into the bed of the truck. He was about to say something to Houston, but just went and sat in the cab next to him. Darnell got in next to John. Houston started the truck and it rolled out into the street.

After two blocks Darnell asked, "Where we goin'?"

"City Hall."

Darnell immediately opened the door. "Hell no! I'm getting' out right here." John grabbed his arm.

■ ● ■

Houston glared at Darnell while making a turn. "Don't open the door while the truck is movin'! I might sideswipe one of these parked cars."

"Well then stop the truck because I am leavin' y'all."

Houston said, "We are gonna need you, Darnell. I don't know if you noticed, but the paint in his hair at the back of his head matches the paint on your basement floor."

Darnell slammed the door shut. "Are you sayin' you gonna jam me up over somethin' I ain't did?!"

"We'll be home in half an hour. Nobody is going to do anything except see some white man dead on the steps of City Hall."

"What about the paint?"

"Now unless someone says where to look, how is anyone going to know where to look?"

"This is blackmail!"

"This is we need your help and you gonna help us because you're our friend."

"Not no more I ain't. I don't need to do no penitentiary time for your friendship. Hell…"

They were all quiet for the next ten minutes. John was wondering what his new cellmate might look like.

As Houston pulled up to the stop sign they all saw him. A police officer had been bent down at a newspaper box and then stood up. He walked through the truck's headlight beams and strolled around to Houston's open window.

"Where you men headin' for?"

"We're takin' our boss home. He had too much to drink after we finished doin' some dry wall and we called his wife and she said bring him on home." The cop moved away from the window and looked in the back. Darnell stuck his head out the window and got sick. John's left leg started going up and down

■ ● ■

like a piston until Houston grabbed his knee to hold it still. The cop moved back to the window.

"You all been drinkin'?"

"No, sir. Just the boss and Joseph, there. The boss said he didn't want to drink alone. We better get him home. His wife gets mean when he gets like this. Last time this happened his wife made us put him out with the chickens."

The cop burst out laughing. "All night?! Out in the shed?!" Houston nodded yes. "You better get him on home then. I sure would like to see that." The cop suddenly got straight faced. "Hope I never get hitched to a woman like that. Damn. Okay. Better take him on home then."

Houston made a right turn and drove down the street at the speed limit. John was staring at him.

"What?"

"So you put that pillow under his head. Put the blanket over him. Made him look like he was passed out. Put that bottle of whiskey in his hand and brought us down here with the chance of us getting pulled over by cops. So far you got a great plan. Now what are we going to do? He's going to remember us when someone finds the body."

"I doubt it. You think that young peckerwood is going to say anything to anybody when the body is found. The three of us fooled that white boy and he's gonna say what? If they don't throw him off the police force, that kind of thing will be in his ear for about the rest of his career. He ain't gonna say nothin'. Darnell! Keep your head out the window. I don't want you sick in my cab."

When Houston pulled the truck up to the curb at City Hall they all swiveled their heads to see if anyone was around.

John said, "Get out, Darnell."nDarnell didn't move. "Get

■ ● ■

out, Darnell. Open the door and get out." John reached across Darnell and opened the door. "Get out." Then John pushed him. Darnell stumbled on the sidewalk. Houston was up in the bed. He had the body hanging over the side.

"Fool! Get over here and help John."

"You help 'em. I can walk from here."

"Darnell, the paint is as clear as day."

Darnell looked up at Houston in a daze. He moved over to the truck to help John. They dragged the dead man over to the City Hall steps and set him down.

"Put him up one more step so he is completely in the shadows."

Darnell and John looked at each other. Then they bent over and lifted the man up one more step. He was barely visible now. Darnell walked back to the truck. "Give me the bottle."

"Uh-uh. Don't need no complicating evidence."

Darnell squinted up at Houston. "Gimme the fuckin' bottle!"

Houston stared down at Darnell for a second then bent over, picked up the whiskey bottle and tossed it to Darnell. Darnell took the cap off and sucked the contents out of it.

John shook his head and got back in the cab.

John looked at page three again. A man was found dead on the steps of City Hall. The coroner said it looked like the man had a stroke but he couldn't be sure until there was an autopsy. The deceased had not been identified yet, but police speculated that he was in the construction trades because of the paint they found in his hair.

John put the evening paper down on his kitchen table and went out the back door with a cup of coffee and the new book he was determined to finish that morning. The sun was just coming up and John sat down. He opened his book again to page 57.

■ ● ■

He looked past the railing He read two words and looked up again. He tilted his head to the right to get an angle on what he thought he saw. He stood up, looked over the railing, grabbed it with two hands and said, "Shi-it!"

The dog looked up at him startled. Then it grabbed the dead rabbit in his mouth and took off running past Houston's porch out of sight.

John sat back down. He picked up his book and resisted looking left or right.

■ ● ■

Hiding Behind the Waves

We lived at the edge of the ocean. When the tide would go out I could feel him become anxious. Sometimes he would get upset and from the bedroom window I could see him throw stones angrily into the wet sand at his feet.

But when the tide came in he would seem light-hearted. He would hum a song, grab me around the waist. He'd make me waltz with him over the uneven floorboards until we tripped, stumbled and struggled for balance. After we laughed he would kiss me lightly and then guide me by the hand out to the shore-line to watch the waves lick their way closer to our feet.

Often I could see his eyes dance, and he would exclaim, "Isn't this wonderful?" When I saw him like this the only thing I could say was, "Yes." And then, "Yes," again. I would stare out across the water to a horizon until my eyes needed to see him and then I would turn and feel the same way when I looked at him as when I looked at something as vast as the ocean.

So many days the sky and water would appear gray. But it didn't matter to him if the tide was coming in. From the bed-room window I would sometimes see him clasp his hands on top of his head. Eventually he would turn around with a grin on his

■●■

face. He would stride back to our cottage and I knew he would begin to work at his desk. Sometimes on his way to his writing he would pause in the doorway of his study and say, "Before our story began I've loved you." I would smile and whisper, "I know that." At those moments it would feel like my heart had stolen all of the space my lungs should have and I would find myself gasping for a breath.

I would watch him pick up his pen and settle into his chair and his arm would move the pen like an ocean current. I would feel so calm watching him. It was so wonderful here.

My friend, Elise, sent me a letter that said she wanted to come visit us. I told David and he said that was fantastic. He thought we should pick her up in Ralston. I told him she'd be almost an hour closer if she rode the bus all the way in to Cloverly. He smiled while telling me that if we met her in Ralston we could stop at that country café-bar that I liked so much. Then he added that there was no reason not to get her off a bus an hour sooner to start having a relaxing visit. "So what if we have to drive a couple of hours to get her. The ride back will be worth it."

I thought it was odd of David to want to do this since he hated being in the car for drives that lasted over ninety minutes. But I did like that café, and it would be a nice way to start her visit.

The day Elise was to arrive we managed to get to the Ralston bus stop half an hour early. We stood outside the hardware store/bus depot looking in the window at the power tools and ax handles. Or at least, I did. David paced back and forth with a smile on his face. At one point he stopped, stared at me and told me he wished we'd brought the camera. "You look great." I pushed the braid that was hanging partially across my face behind my ear and shrugged. Then he started pacing again.

Elise's visit was like a tonic. I didn't realize how much I had missed her until we were at the café. David said he'd only have one beer so that the two of us could get drunk if we wanted to. It was then Elise announced that she was pregnant.

I screeched, "What?!" I knocked my silverware to the floor. The waitress came over and asked us if the water was okay. David thought that was hilarious. I was hugging Elise when I heard David say, "Sorry for the commotion, boys. I'm going to be a father."

My head snapped in David's direction. I felt like I was staring at him through a long, dark tunnel. Then I looked at Elise. She had a deep frown on her face. She glanced at me and turned back to David, just as four burly men got up from their table and invaded ours. They slapped him on the back, shook his shoulders and then the shots started coming. Elise was looking at me in wide-eyed confusion. I was just about to end David's celebration but instead I started laughing. The men were now congratulating Elise, shaking her hand; asking if they had any names picked out. She was having a hard time saying thank you.

I couldn't stop laughing. One of the men asked me if I wanted a shot. I said no and he asked if I was pregnant too. I shook my head. "No, no, no. I'm driving." Elise suddenly burst out laughing with her arm raised to her mouth. She'd finally caught on that David's 'fatherhood' was a ploy to get a free drunk on.

David had now moved to the burly-man table. They were all discussing first names based on football linebackers. Elise and I sat close to each other at our own table holding hands. First names hadn't come up yet.

"I'm not going to live with him."

"Will that be hard, Elise?"

■ ● ■

"Maybe. But I don't love him. Not really. At first I thought I did. But I guess that might have been my way of escaping from the life we used to have."

"Well, regardless of what happens, or whatever you do, I'm always there for you."

"Always?"

"Always."

"What if I need fourteen years of babysitting at some point?"

"Don't you have any other friends?! I can only guarantee twelve."

Elise scrunched her face up like I had wretchedly bad breath. "Some friend."

"Don't try to guilt me!" Elise looked beautiful and I wanted to hug her. What will you do for work?"

She shrugged. If I live frugally I'll have more than enough money to cover the next four years. The severance turned out good. What about you?"

"I haven't taken mine yet."

I felt Elise's body shift. "Oh! I didn't realize…"

"No, no. I'm taking it. I'm done. I just don't want it yet. It's still there. I'm definitely taking it."

David started snoring in the back seat.

"Does he snort and rumble like that whenever he sleeps?"

I chuckled. "No. Just when he gets really drunk. Hey! Jerk-face!"

"Wha…"Then it was quiet in the back seat again.

Elise giggled while looking over her shoulder. "Wow. That's like magic."

"I learned that by accident one night when he was really pissing me off. Four o'clock in the morning and he's sounding like a coal-burning locomotive. It works every time. Have no idea why."

■ ● ■

Elise and I took long walks every day. We spent a lot of time talking about the past and almost as much about the future and babies. Two weeks later, when Elise left, David acted like the tide had gone out and he didn't expect it to come back in for a very long time. It was almost like Elise was security for us. She'd brought a favorite childhood blanket that covered all three of us.

One night at dinner David suddenly said, "That visit with Elise was really nice." After that he was kind of back to normal, shifting from moody to ebullient.

One afternoon we were shopping for our weekly supplies at Orville's General Store, Appliances and Coffee Shop. David grabbed my arm and pulled me toward the side door.

"What are you doing?"

"We have to get back home. I…I left the gas on."

"No you didn't."

"Yeah. I think I did."

"So go home and come back for me."

"No. Come with me."

I glanced around the store. Through the front window I saw old John Drago sitting on his favorite barrel. Jane Wheeler was walking by. Across the street I could see two men coming out of the Post Office.

David squeezed my arm tighter. "Please?"

So we went out the side door and drove back to our cottage much faster than usual. I knew I had a smirk on my face as David went through the pantomime of checking the stove. He looked at me like he was ashamed, realizing I saw through his ridiculous performance.

As he moved past me he said, "Sorry. I was wrong. I'll go back for the groceries later." Then he told me he wanted to go back alone. At this point, I was fine with that.

■ ● ■

The next morning when I woke up, David was already gone. I was cleaning a wool sweater in the sink when he walked in.

"Hi." I glanced at him and concentrated on kneading the wet material while admiring the stitch. He started to move toward his studio.

"Is that a gun?"

David was quiet for quite a few moments, standing in the doorway of the kitchen and his study. I assumed he was probably collecting thoughts that had been scattered by my question.

Finally he said, "Yes it is."

I turned from the sink to look at him. "Okay." I wiped my hands on a dish towel. His eyes betrayed a fear I had never seen there before. Was it my disapproval or something else?

"We're kind of isolated out here, aren't we?" He nodded. "Does it make you feel better to have one in the house?"

"Yes. I think it will."

"Okay." I put the dish towel down and crossed my arms on my chest. "You know, you haven't taken me dancing in quite some time…do you think you could take me dancing?"

David snatched at his escape. "Yeah. We could do that." He finally moved out of the doorway and slipped into his study.

We went dancing. David loved slow-dancing. But this night he held me closer than he usually did. It felt like he was trying to remember who I was.

When we got home he walked around outside for few minutes. He ended up wandering into our bedroom and making love to me like it was the first time we ever met.

Two evenings later we were having an unusually quiet dinner. David had helped me with cooking, but had hardly said anything.

■ ● ■

I watched him in the candle light. He looked up and gave me that lovely smile he seemed to save for me.

"David, are we hiding?"

He looked back down at his food. "I'm not real hungry. I'll just save this. I'm going down to the water. After you're done, come down if you want. It would be nice if you did."

I watched him start out the door.

"David, are we here because we're hiding? I think it's lovely living out here, but is that the reason you wanted to live out here?"

David turned to look at me for a second and then he went out the door. I saw him pass the kitchen window with the twilight behind him.

I wasn't going to force David to answer my question, though in my heart I knew he already had. I wondered who David thought we were hiding from. I wondered what David thought was going on. If I couldn't get the answer to "are we hiding?" I doubted he was going to answer any of my other questions.

On a Saturday morning David flew into the driveway. He slammed the car door. He ran past me into the house. He came out holding the gun. I grabbed his arm with both hands.

"David, give that to me."

Our eyes met and I could see the fear he had been carrying around for days.

"David…" I took the gun from his grasp and walked around the corner of the cottage. I surveyed the dunes. I started off to the left. I could feel him staring at my back as I slipped over the first dune.

It was warm that day. I looked down once at the sand pushing its way in between my toes. I brushed a wrinkle out of my skirt. I sighed, looked up at a two-tone grey sky and kept walking.

■ ● ■

There were two shots. I staggered once, then started heading back for home. Maybe I should have worn shoes before I left. When I was at the top of the dune I could see David standing at the corner of the cottage. He had a knife in his hand. I walked across the sand to him slowly, faintly smiling, trying to look re-assuring. When I was in front of him I ran my hand across the side of his face.

"You have to trust me. Okay?"

He nodded, dropped the knife and pulled me into his arms.

"Before our story started I've loved you."

I whispered. "I know."

He squeezed me and squeezed me again. I wanted to cry when I finally looked in his eyes.

"Can you start dinner? I'm going to be a little while. I have to do something."

I went to the back of the cottage and grabbed my shoes and a shovel. As I went past David I rubbed his arm.

"Don't forget to take the knife back inside. You might need it for the carrots. You should go down to the water. The tide will be coming in."

He finally gave me a slight smile as I glanced back over my shoulder. I walked back over the dune dragging the shovel behind me and looking at the pattern it made in the sand.

■ ● ■

Duke

I took my rifle from the wall, went out the door and was greeted by Duke. Fourteen years old now, he had met me at the door thousands of times. His tail wagged almost like it always had only slower. I brushed my hand over his ears and we set off down the path like we had so many times before.

I could see Duke as a young dog full of energy. Running to the right. Sniffing. Running back to the left, scrounging through the brush.

Now he limped and every few feet he stumbled a little. Once he looked back at me as if to apologize for being old.

The woods were the same. The occasional wood thrush would sing. A blue jay would scream. The path was remarkably clear even though Duke and I were the only ones to use it these days. The sun broke through the leaves here and there. For some reason it reminded me of our old tree fort that by now had fallen out of the trees.

When we got to the cliff I looked down into the gorge to the stream. It was sparkling and noisy. Duke sat down looking across the gorge to the other side. A hawk swept through the opening. Duke and I watched it glide away. I looked down at Duke with

■ ● ■

the sun shining on his fur. For a moment he looked like the young dog that had gone on so many little adventures with me. Then Duke looked up at me almost saying, "What now?" When Duke turned away I said, "Goodbye."

The walk out of the woods was lonely. Not as bad as I thought it would be. Now I'd have to go find the shovel.

■ ● ■

George

"Sammy, your father is coming up the stairs."

Sammy ran to the doorway of his room and put his hands on each side of the door jamb.

George came through the open kitchen door and placed a kiss on his wife's lips while she stood at the stove preparing dinner.

George turned to his son and said, "Samson!"

Sammy ran across the kitchen yelling "Jurge!" His father picked Sammy up under his

arms and lifted him toward the ceiling quickly. Sammy squealed with excitement.

"Jurge! Do it again!" George repeated the lift again and again. Until Sara said "Y'all go wash your hands, now. Time for dinner."

"C'mon Samson. We have to wash up."

Sammy led the way to the bathroom and stepped up on a stool next to the sink. George turned on the water checking with one finger to make sure it was not too hot. Sammy mimicked his father and then picked up the soap.

When George and Sam came out of the bathroom, Sammy jumped on his parent's bed which was across from the kitchen

■ ● ■

table against the wall.

"Sammy, you know you're not supposed to jump on that bed." George put his arm around Sammy's waste and picked him up. "Sam, your mother and I told you before you are not allowed to jump on our bed. You know that, right?"

"Yes. Sorry."

"Okay then. Get in your high chair."

"I want to sit at the big table with you and Mom."

"You're too little yet," said Sara

"No I'm not. I can sit like this."

Sara laughed. "That's not sitting. That's kneeling."

"So I can be kneeling. What's kneeling?"

"What you're doing right now.

"Sammy, get down for a second."

"Please can I be at the big table? Please?"

Sammy looked up at George and then climbed down from the chair. George pulled the chair away from the table and placed two phone books on the seat. He then lifted Sam up and told him to sit on the phone books and pushed the chair up to the table. Sammy wiped a single tear from his cheek with his left hand and broke into a wide grin.

Sara served the plates with chicken, sweet potatoes and dandelion greens.

"How was work today?"

"Not as bad as usual."

"The union men still talking?"

"Yes…I think they consider me a union man."

"Oh George…Aren't most of them communists?"

"A lot of them are I think."

"What if you lose your job?"

"I'll have to find another one. But I think we can win."

"I hope so."

■ ● ■

"What's a yun yun , Jurge?"

"It when people at a factory get together to make things better."

Sara looked at George with a slight smile on her face.

George smiled back and said "Tomorrow we're going to the zoo."

Sara was stunned. "By ourselves?!"

"No, with some of the union men from the factory.

Is that a good idea? What if there's another riot?"

"Sam will be able to see lions and giraffes."

"Real lions?" Sammy was clearly excited.

"That's right."

"What's a yiraff?"

"That's the animal with the really long neck like the picture in your coloring book. You'll see one tomorrow." After I do the dishes you get in your pajamas and pick out a book and I'll read it to you."

Sammy ran to his bedroom, took off his shirt and looked down into the street. Lots of people were walking by since it was Saturday. Sam waved at some people who did not wave back.

"Sam, when that window is open, I don't want you to go close to it.

"I was waving at people, Jurge."

"Did you hear me Sammy? I don't want you falling out the window and banging your head on the sidewalk. Did you hear me Sammy?"

"Yes."

"What are we reading?"

"The I think I can book."

"The *Little Engine That Could*. That's a good one."

"I counted my books. I have eight."

"You have eight books? How did you learn to count that high?

■ ● ■

"My mom showed me how!"

"Show me. Let's see."

Sammy proudly counted each book up to eight and stacked them neatly.

"Good work, Samson. Now let's read your book."

Sammy fell asleep on page two.

George walked out into the kitchen. "Sara! What are you doing to that boy during the day? He's out already."

Sara smiled and put down a copy of 'The Defender' on the table. She stood up and hugged her husband.

George rolled over and put his bare feet on the cracked linoleum floor. He stared at Sara who was making coffee.

"Good morning Ms. Sara, the honey in my hive."

"Don't start talking silly so early in the morning."

"Can't help myself sometimes." George yawned. "I'm going to shave before we leave." George walked to the bathroom.

"Oh my lord! What was that?! Was that a gun?"

George wiped shaving soap from his face while stepping out of the bathroom. "Sounded like a gun. First thing in the morning. Damn!"

Sammy, come out here and eat some breakfast so we can go to the zoo."

Sammy walked into the kitchen with a blanket wrapped around his shoulders.

"Sammy, what are you doing with that blanket? Take it back to the bed."

Sammy stood in the kitchen staring at his mother. Sara walked over to him and pulled the blanket. "Let go of the blanket, Sam."

"Blood! George! Sammy is bleeding!"

George rushed into the room.

"What happened?"

■ ● ■

"I don't know, George. I'll run downstairs and call the ambulance."

"I'll take him myself. Take the ambulance too long in our neighborhood. Get me a towel, Sara."

George made a compress and put it on Sammy's stomach, wrapped him in the blanket, picked him up and raced down the stairs.

"I'm sorry Jurge. I'm tired."

"Right now you stay awake Samson. Stay awake."

"I feel funny, Jurge."

"You just stay awake."

George ran through an intersection ignoring the screams of car horns.

"I'm sorry. Don't be mad at me. I won't do it again."

"Won't do what?"

"I got too close to the window. You told me not to. I'm sorry, Jurge. I won't do it again. I feel sleepy. Can I go to sleep now?"

"Not yet Sammy. "

"Okay, Jurge."

Sammy's eyes closed.

"Wake up Sammy. We're almost there."

George could see the hospital less than a block away.

George ran into the emergency room. A man yelled at him." You can't come in here!"

"My son has been shot."

"Don't matter."

"I've got him Johnson. Nurse Henry. We need a gurney here immediately!"

"We can't have every colored in Chicago just coming in here whenever they like."

"It's okay this time Johnson." The doctor laid Sammy on the

gurney and it was wheeled away.

"You sit over there. Johnson pointed to a chair in the corner of the room. George sat down terrified.

The doctor approached George who was still sitting in the corner while Johnson stared at him. George looked up. The doctor sat down next to George.

"How old was your son?"

Tears began to stream down George's face. George glared at the doctor.

"He was three. He was only three!"

"I'm really sorry." The doctor stood up. Johnson moved toward George.

"You get away from me you cracker son of a bitch."

The doctor waved Johnson away.

"Do you have a wife?" George didn't respond. "Go home to your wife. Your wife will need you."

George climbed the stairs like he always did.

Sara was sitting at the kitchen table. "Where's Sammy?"

George stayed silent. "George! Where's Sammy?"George could hear the panic in her voice.

"He's gone, Sara. He gone."

"What you mean He's gone? What does that mean?!" Sara stood up.

"He died."

"You let our son die?!"

"No, I didn't let him die! Someone shot him."

Sara sat down again crying with her head resting on her folded arms.

"I'm going for a walk. Do you want to come with me?"

"No! I'm not sharing my grief with that world out there."

■ ● ■

"George was angry that Sara had said he let Sammy die. He was torn between staying with Sara and getting away from her.

"I'll be back in a little while. I'll get some food so you don't cook today."

Sara stayed silent.

George went to work the next day. Sara said she would work out arrangements with the Reverend. George didn't say anything.

George felt everyone was staring. He looked around the room. He continued to shovel animal parts into a pile. For the first time on his job he could smell the blood. He watched it run down the trough into the drain. At the end of the day he walked over to the creek. It always ran red, except on Monday mornings. Then it was pink until noon.

George started toward home thinking it was hot out. Very hot. He had to get away from the heat. He saw Sara packing a bag.

"Sara,…what are you doing?"

"Leaving George. I can't be here."

"Forever?"

"Yes. Forever."

"Do you want me to come with you?"

"You can stay here. I think you can live in this violence. I can't."

"Sara…"

"Don't say anything else George. It'over"

"What?!"

"Don't raise your voice. That don't change anything. Maybe you and the union men can figure something out.

■ ● ■

George walked over to the top of the stairs and watched Sara walk down them through the shadows. When she pushed the downstairs door open she looked like she was engulfed in light and then she disappeared. George knew he would do something.

George began to walk faster. He passed the fruit stand that had very sweet oranges. He walked quickly past the butcher shop. He saw a headline about the Kefauver commission. He began to run. As he passed the barber shop someone called out to him, "George." He began to run faster. The street became a blur as he dodged people coming home from work. It crossed his mind that he had good work shoes. He was almost out of breath when he slammed through the downstairs door. He ran up the stairs two at a time.

"George. You're home a little early. Are you okay, hon?" George mimed 'Yes with his head nodding back and forth toward the floor. "Is it that hot outside? You're very sweaty. Whyn't you take a shower before dinner?"

"Jurge!" Sammy ran across the kitchen and slammed into George's leg. George lifted Sammy up, squeezed him to his chest and whispered, "Samson."

■●■

Janis

I felt like I was standing in a cesspool of bad memories. Across the street she was up on her tiptoes hollering and waving at me. I returned half a wave somewhat reluctantly. When I started to step off the curb to keep going, she screamed, "Wait up!" My stomach contracted as she dodged her way through traffic while I imagined the sound of a car's impact with her body.

She had been hit by a car once when I was with her. I was about ten feet behind her. The driver had backed up without looking while she was already waiting to cross the street. The driver had gotten out and screamed at her for touching his car. I was immediately ready to fight and began yelling at him. She had grabbed my arm and held me back saying she was really okay. The driver looked at me, jumped back in his car and pulled out. I wrote down the license plate number and was prepared to call the police. Instead, she took the note from me, crumpled it up, tossed it away and limped across the street with me holding her arm.

"Hey!" She still had the infectious smile and it was nice to know that my inoculation was still good.

"Didn't expect to see me, did ya'?"

■ ● ■

I spared her half a smile. "No, Janis. I guess not."

"Where ya' heading to?" She started looking around while I tried to come up with a lie.

"You're going to that coffee shop on the next block, aren't ya'? Let me go with you."

"I'm not going to be there very long. I'm just going to get a coffee."

"Well, let me buy you one. C'mon. I need one too. C'mon. It won't be that bad."

I wasn't sure about that. I was heading into a depressing afternoon, that in my imagination, now had the possibility of being much, much worse.

I looked at her face beaming at me, a lot like when we first met. I sighed and said, "Yes. Okay."

"Good. We can catch up with each other."

Janis bounced along beside me chattering about the weather, wondering when the sun would be out again. I thought about how little I wanted her to know about my current life, and how I was going to keep it that way.

When we were close to the coffee shop she quickened her pace so that she could open the door for me. I paused at the entrance until she waved me in with a half bow and an "apres vous."

I shook my head slightly, entered and went to a table by the window. Janis threw her jacket over the back of a chair like she was settling in for the afternoon. Then she sat down across from me just beaming. I stared out the window remaining silent while she said a few things about me and the décor.

"Is this your regular spot? This could get depressing, ya' know."

I glanced at her and turned my head back to the window.

"Look…if you really don't want me here, just say so. I can leave."

■ ● ■

"You said you were paying. Prices too steep?"

She laughed.

"Naw. I think I can afford this. So really…is this someplace you hang out in a lot?"

I looked at her smirk and felt disgusted.

"No. Only when I'm on my way to a funeral."

Her face lost the beam.

"Oh. I'm sorry. Who died?"

I looked out the window and said, "David Creller."

"Holy shit. He died? Died of what? He's your age, isn't he?"

I looked at her again like she was a babbling child.

"I didn't mean to say you're old. He was young. What'd he die from?"

"He was murdered."

Janis started looking around the coffee shop. She rapped her knuckles on the table twice.

"I'm going to track down a couple of cups of coffee from our speedy waitress and then you can tell me all about it."

She jumped up like she was escaping. And then I realized she was. She looked really uncomfortable when I told her David had been murdered. I watched her harass the waitress behind the counter, both hands gesticulating, fingers spread, beseeching. She was trying to regain her composure by agitating someone else. I'd seen her do this before quite a few times. It was embarrassing at the beginning of our relationship. Then it became a curiosity and I would just watch her perform. It was a performance that gave her space from the tension she was trying to escape from.

I watched her turn around with a coffee in each hand. As she came back to our table she raised her eyebrows like she had accomplished something very important.

"Cream, no sugar…right?"

■ ● ■

"Correct."

"Good memory, right? So how did David get murdered? Not like it's a shock the way he was living."

"Someone shot him in the head three times and then cut off his head, or someone cut off his head and then shot him three times."

"Are you serious? Someone cut off his head?! With what? A scimitar or something?"

"A chainsaw."

"What?!"

She seemed genuinely shocked. She stared at me wide-eyed and then her eyes narrowed to slits.

"How do you know that? I didn't hear about that. The news rags usually pick up on something gruesome like that."

"His sister and his mother told me."

"Oh, boy. What a pair. Where did you run into them?"

"They called me. David had my number in his pocket. The police came to my apartment to talk to me and apparently the cops gave them my number as one of his friends."

"When was the last time you saw him? It was a while ago wasn't it? And where do you live now?"

Janis had this characteristic of trying to run two or three conversation subjects at the same time. I could see that hadn't changed, but I was going to shut one of them down right now.

"About three years ago and I live on Boyle, but let's just finish the conversation about David, okay?"

"Do you really want to know why I left you?"

"Don't really care."

She looked down at the table and then raised her head with an almost pious look on her face.

"Being with you was like being in a foreign country during a perfect season. I had to go because nothing had been so perfect

■ ● ■

before. I had to leave before I ruined it. I ruin everything and somewhere in my life I need to have something, some place, some thing that I know was good, that I can look back on and think, 'that was a perfect time, something perfectly good.' I had to go before I ruined it."

I wanted to say 'you should have tried to stay longer. Maybe with a little practice life would have been perfect.' But I bit my tongue because I knew in my heart, from her viewpoint, it was probably true. From my perspective she had screwed me up for a fairly long time. But even if she was right, I couldn't let what she said just pass.

"Very poetic. But guess what? I have to leave or I'll ruin my afternoon. Have a funeral to go to."

I got up and walked to the door thinking I shouldn't have been so rude. I should at least say 'goodbye.' I stretched my arm out to leave an overly generous tip on the front counter for the waitress who had taken Janis's abuse. My arm almost hit Janis in the chest.

"Sorry."

Janis looked at the money I had dropped in the tip bowl.

"Damn…was I that bad?"

"From the look on the waitress's face, I'd say 'yeah.'"

I went out on the sidewalk and with my back turned said, "See ya'." I took about four steps and realized Janis was now walking right next to me. I stopped and looked at her.

"Where the hell are you going?"

Janis looked around like she was trying to get her bearings and then nonchalantly said, "The funeral."

"What? Why are you going to David's funeral?"

She looked at me like I had said someone was eating a shit sandwich somewhere and we were going to go watch.

"I knew him, too. It's not like I didn't know him. You can't stop me from going to his funeral, if that's what you're thinking."

She started looking around again. She crossed her arms, frowned at me, then looked away. "If we don't get going, we're going to be late, aren't we?"

"You don't even know what time it starts."

"Well, inside you said you had to get going and I know how you never want to be late for anything…except a really good party. You never minded being late for one of those."

That really pissed me off. I stopped.I glared at her, but I wasn't going to rehash old conflicts after all of these years. I turned and started walking. Janis fell in beside me like our stroll to the funeral parlor had been planned all along.

"It's about the rent, right?"

"What the hell are you talking about?

"I stuck you with a big rent when I left."

"That's past. I don't even think about it."

"Well, I'll make it up to you."

"You bought me a coffee. That's good enough."

"But you didn't drink it. How far is it to David's funeral?"

I ignored her question and started to think about the times Janis and David had gotten together. It was like fire and gasoline. Once, David had been driving so recklessly, that I told him to stop the car so I could walk home. Janis begged me to stay. "We're just having some fun." I got out, watchedDavid burn rubber as he pulled away, fishtailing down the street. An hour later I was looking out my apartment window when David's car slid around the corner and stopped out front. A police car with its lights flashing came around the corner to stop at the back of David's car. Then another police car came from the opposite direction to block David in. And then there was Janis, running for my apartment building's front door with a bag in her hand. I could hear someone yelling "Stop right there." I ran to the buzz-

■ ● ■

er to let her in the building. I opened the door and listened to her take the stairs two at a time. She flew through my door and went straight to the kitchen. I heard the freezer door open and slam closed. Then Janis ran right back to the front door. Out of breath she said, "I better get back down there. I didn't want the ice cream to melt."

Out in the hallway Janis stepped into the arms of a police officer who didn't care when she told him she had intended to come right back down. As he was putting cuffs on her she said, "Can you post bail for me if it's necessary? I don't want to bother my father. You like cherry, right?"

"What?"

"Cherry. Cherry Vanilla. In the freezer."

I ended up bailing David and Janis out the next day. We came back to my apartment and they started eating the ice cream, talking about the previous night's fiasco like it was a Peter Pan adventure.

"So someone really cut off his head?"

"Apparently."

"How long have you lived on Boyle?"

"A couple of years."

"What number? Maybe I can stop by sometime."

"Unlisted."

"What? What's unlisted?"

"My address."

"I'll pay you back."

"Will you forget about it…it's a long time ago…it's finished."

We walked in silence for another whole block.

"Why would someone cut off David's head? I mean, they shot him. Wouldn't that be good enough?"

"I don't know. Maybe sending someone a message. Maybe it

was just a guy who was crazy."

"Or a woman."

"A woman probably would have used a carving knife."

"Probably right. Want to know where I live?"

"Not really."

"Philadelphia. Are you still a surveyor?"

"What are you doing here?"

Janis frowned. "I thought you didn't like that?"

I frowned. "Don't like what?"

"When we have two or three conversations going at the same time."

"What are you talking about?! You said you lived in Philadelphia and I wondered what you were doing here?"

"Yeah. But that's like three or four things. I still don't know if you're a surveyor. You never really asked me if I liked where I live and that's different from me explaining why I'm here. And, we were talking about a carving knife. A man can use a carving knife, too."

I looked at Janis with a sympathetic smile in one corner of my mouth. I wondered if she was really starting to lose her mind.

"I'm also reading 'Dialectical Ontology' by…"

"How do you like living in Philadelphia?"

"It's great. I really like it there. I'm here to see my aunt. Everybody else is either dead or they moved away. Some great clubs to hear music in. Think any of the guys who did the deed will be there?"

"Sometimes I think you're autistic." I turned right and pointed to Pascarelli's Funeral Home about a block and a half away.

"Who's paying for this anyways?"

"I don't know. Maybe he had insurance. Maybe a few of the guys he ran around with."

When we went in the front door it was like a wave of the

■ ● ■

patois of the Caribbean Islands washed over us. I recognized the first man I saw in the hallway. I extended my hand and watched his dreads sway back and forth as he grabbed my hand.

"Michael…how are you? Long time."

"Sad day, mon. Sad day."

From behind me I heard Janis introduce herself and then introduce herself again in French. I moved down the hall toward the viewing room, realizing most of the people here seemed to be West Indian. A scattering of white faces in a sea of brown. All here to see David, with his long blond dreads.

David's mother, sister and an uncle I had met once, were standing off to the right of the casket. I went to pay my respects to the family and heard laughter erupting from the hallway. I turned around just in time to see Janis come into the room with a big smile on her face, followed by four or five men, all of who were smiling. As soon as Janis saw me, her smile disappeared.

I said 'hello' to David's mother and sister, shook hands with the uncle and then moved over by the casket. Out of the corner of my eye I saw Janis hug all three of them like she had know them all of her life. I looked down at David in heavy makeup. His head looked distorted, misshapen.

I was thinking that I had known David twenty-six years. The last seven I hardly saw him other than to say "what's up?" I was glad I had cut my ties to him, if only so I didn't feel close to him right now.

Some kids used to call us "Salt and Pepper." Not very original, but the tag caught on. Then David started getting really stupid. He got caught in a burglary and managed to get probation. He thought it was a good deal. He told me he had done about ten burglaries before he'd gotten caught. His sister opened a bank account for him, so he thought he was way ahead. Now, he said, he had seed money for his future investments. He looked

■ ● ■

so serious when he added, "Just like the Kennedys."

"His neck looks short, doesn't it?"

I jumped a little. I didn't expect Janis to be on my left. David was wearing a dark turtleneck sweater under his jacket and his neck did look short. But then a chainsaw probably didn't leave an even cut.

I grabbed Janis's wrist and whispered, "What the hell are you doing?!"

"I want to see the scar. Don't you?"

"No. I don't."

Janis shook my hand free and reached for David's collar again. I slapped her hand and then looked around quickly to see if anyone was watching our little pantomime. One man on the other side of the room was looking at us with eyebrows raised.

"Let's sit down. You can't examine a body at a funeral!"

"Well, he's going to be gone soon…"

I grabbed her arm. "Let's sit down!"

"Okay. Okay. You lead the way."

I let go of her arm and started down the middle aisle. I turned to go into the fourth row and realized that Janis was back at the casket. Someone else was standing next to her. I sat down noticing that the man with the raised eyebrows was still watching me. Janis gave the person next to her a hug and then Janis was alone at the casket again. I saw her look to her left and right and slowly she leaned over the body.

She straightened, then turned around with tears in her eyes. As she moved toward me I could see the man with raised eyebrows was watching her. He shook his head and waved at her. She waved back and sat down beside me.

"How was the scar?"

"They made it very even-looking."

"What the hell is wrong with you?"

■ ● ■

Then I noticed the man with raised eyebrows was sitting right next to Janis. I also noticed that Janis had not wiped the tears away.

"I saw you kiss him goodbye. Were you a good friend of his?"

Janis's mouth opened and nothing came out. She looked toward the casket, wiped her eyes and then said, "Yes. But Christian, here, was friends with David for over twenty years."

The man looked past Janis to me. It seemed his eyebrows were in a constant state of arousal.

"Really?" He seemed incredulous.

Janis said, "Really. They went to school together and grew up together."

"So why haven't I met you before?"

"Uhh…I guess we went into different circles after a while."

"I can understand that. We grow older and sometimes we grow apart, but the old memories are still there."

"Yeah. Plus he liked being around police more than I did."

Janis caught her breath. The man's eyebrows fell and he stared at me. I almost apologized until the man broke out laughing.

"I know what you mean. David was like a magnet for the police. He knew all the cops by their first names. I'm Michael, by the way." He held out his hand to shake.

"Oh. There's my wife. David loved her goat water."

"So you're not from here?"

"Oh, yes. I'm from here, but my wife is from Montserrat. Excuse me. I'm going to go back and join her. And sister, you stay strong." He patted her arm and moved back to the other side of the room to be with his wife. They started whispering. I looked back toward the casket. The rows of seats were almost all full except for some of the ones in front of us. The first row had David's family. The second row had a few men with really long dreads. There was no one directly in front of us.

■ ● ■

Janis elbowed me in the ribs. I turned toward her.

"What?"

"Michael's wife is trying to get your attention."

I looked around Janis to see Michael's wife wave at me. I waved back. I took the opportunity to glance behind me. Every seat was taken with some people standing all the way at the back.

The minister walked slowly into the room from the right. He ended up hovering over the casket. The room went completely silent. The minister was wearing glasses and the reflection of light made it impossible to see his eyes. He put a hand on the casket. He began to slowly shake his head. It occurred to me that I didn't expect the minister to be black. I thought David's family would have a minister from their own church. On the other hand, maybe he was the minister of their church.

In a room completely silent, of course Janis would have something to say even if it was a whisper.

"For how he lived his life, he really built up a community of friends."

"Shh."

"I'm whispering."

I whispered back. "Don't care."

From behind me I heard a woman's voice say, "You right, honey. David had a whole community of people he loved and who loved him." A hand appeared on Janis's shoulder and patted it a few times.

The minister moved away from the casket and put his arms out holding a bible in his left hand. It seemed like he was just about to speak when they came.

The first one came in the same way the minister had. He was dressed completely in black with a black ski mask over his face. He walked past the minister right to the casket. The minister's

■ ● ■

head turned to his left. When the man in black went behind him the minister turned his head to the right to watch him. It was probably then that the minister saw the MAC 9. His arms fell to his side. Two more men with automatics walked in with their weapons lowered on the congregation. Everybody might have stayed seated and calm, but when the minister cried, "O' Lord!" and ran down the center aisle, all hell broke loose. I could hear chairs turning over. People were screaming. A man in front of us started hurdling the rows, never hitting the back of a single one. Two of the men in front of us bolted for the side door. One of them fell over a chair. When he got up the chair lifted off the floor. One of his locks was stuck in the side of the folding chair, so he made it out of the room holding the chair in one hand, while tugging on his dread with the other.

I looked over my shoulder and in the back another man, also all in black, was standing by the back row with a sawed off shot gun. The first man in black was bent over the casket with his arms in it. He seemed to be looking for something. One of the men in black yelled, "Hurry up, God Damn it!" Then the man with the shot gun walked quickly to the front.

"Yeah! Hurry up because now we have trouble."

I noticed Janis turn around. She was staring. She turned around and clasped her hands in her lap. "Oh shit."

I looked behind us. There were men and at least one woman creeping into the room with every kind of weapon I could imagine. The four men in front of us spread out like they were ready to shoot it out.

"Janis. We need to slowly get on the floor." I began to slip off my chair. Janis immediately stood up.

"What are you doing?! Get on the floor!"

She looked down at me. "Shush." She raised her head. "Hey, buddy! Yeah, you."

■ ● ■

Janis tossed him a brown paper bag.

"Now slip out the back so nobody gets hurt." I raised myself back onto my chair. Janis turned toward the rear. "Okay?"

No one said anything. The four men started moving backwards toward a door I couldn't see, but assumed would be there. They disappeared and then everyone was talking all at once. I turned to the back again. The men who had weapons were leaving, probably to put their things back before the police arrived. I suddenly felt stupid. The police were not going to arrive this time. Maybe they'd hear about this in a few weeks, but not today.

Janis sat back down. I looked at her and then back at the casket.

"So why didn't you run?"

"Because you didn't…I thought I should do what you did. Why didn't you run?"

"I guess I got caught up in watching. What was in the bag?"

"I thought you didn't like two strains of a conversation going on at the same time."

I laughed. "What was in the damn bag?"

"I don't know. I thought some disrespectful jerk put their coffee cup in the bag and then dropped it in the casket as a final disrespect to David."

"Let's go outside for second." I lead the way out thinking about the coffee cup explanation. On the way we passed some people coming back in. I heard one man say, "That was some shit!" Somebody else said, "You damn right. Those boys was ready to get hurt." A woman in a black hat was telling three men that her piece was staying in her pocket book. Outside the minister was pacing back and forth, his Bible clasped in both hands. There were women and men keeping right in step, telling him they had to have a service since he had already been paid. A little ways beyond him I saw a UPS man walking through the

■●■

crowd clearly asking questions. Some people shrugged and then I saw Michael's wife point at me. A few people turned around. And then about six or seven people were pointing at me. The UPS man walked up to me and sullenly said I had to sign for the package. I looked at him like he was crazy. He jabbed the pen and board at me and he looked at me like I was half an idiot. I signed and took the package, which turned out to be a letter.

"You get all of your mail at the funeral home now?"

I shared the look I gave the UPS man with Janis while I ran my finger under the envelope flap. Janis started speaking in French to two women who approached her.

I flipped open the single page. *I'm not going to make it out of this one. I really screwed up this time. I made a deal to get this to you. You're probably the only one I can completely trust. I need to let my Moms know that everything is okay and everything has been worked out. Just want you to know you were a really good running partner when we were friends. I kinda got to go. Crazy times. You ever see that woman Janis around? David'*

Janis stopped speaking in French to the women who had approached her and turned her attention back to me.

"What was that?"

"Do me a favor. I'm not going back in. Give David's mother a message. Tell her everything has been worked out."

"Why don't you do it? His mother's a jerk. I don't want to talk to her."

"Yeah, I know. But I'm not going back in there. I'll just say goodbye right here. Good luck in Philly. Do me the favor."

"Yeah, sure, okay. But at least let me give you a goodbye hug."

She wrapped her arms around me squeezed me tight, then grabbed my jacket at the waistline and shook it.

"Probably won't ever be seeing you in Philadelphia, will I?"

"Probably not. Don't want to ruin a perfect season."

■ ● ■

"Yeah. In some foreign country."

She let go of me and walked into the crowd. I saw Michael's wife put her arm around Janis's arm and start talking.

I turned away. I walked four or five blocks trying to see the perfect season from Janis's perspective. I stopped at a traffic light with a funny feeling growing in my stomach. Janis was very intelligent. I found her very sexy. Mostly she was fun to be with. I stopped mid-block with my stomach climbing to my throat. I looked around to make sure no one was close. I put my hands in my jacket pockets. I pulled out the left hand and found five small plastic packets filled with a white powder. I walked over to a trash can, lifted the lid, dropped the packets down the side so they'd fall to the bottom. Then, I put the lid back on the perfect season. Almost ruined. Almost.

■ ● ■

A Green Dinner Murder

Elsa Landreth stepped down off the train at 9:08 a.m. She looked around the platform hoping to see the old yellow sign that pointed toward the taxi stand. She shifted her little gray suitcase to her left hand, took two steps and heard her name.

"Elsa?"

Elsa turned to see police officer Jerry Skinner walking directly at her. She put her suitcase down, getting mentally ready for a confrontation.

"Elsa. Elsa Landreth."

Elsa nodded, but didn't look Skinner in the face.

"Where are you headed for?"

"I'm off parole. I can go anywhere I want to and I don't have to answer your questions."

Skinner put both hands up shoulder-high, like he was signaling his surrender.

"Whoa…I'm sorry. I was thinking I haven't seen you in close to ten years. I thought I'd just say something to you and maybe offer to give you a ride if you need one."

"You don't think Toby would let me sit in his cab? Or is this just idle, fat ass law enforcement curiosity?"

■ ● ■

The smile collapsed from Skinner's face.

"Look…first of all Toby doesn't drive any more. A little too old for that these days. I can't pretend I'm not curious. You've been gone such a long time. I heard a rumor that you were at Luthorn College."

Elsa looked at the officer and folded her arms over her chest. "Yeah…so?!"

Skinner started to feel embarrassed. He looked around the platform to see who might be watching.

"So nothing really, but if you are, I think that's great."

They stared at each other. Elsa was determined not to speak next. Skinner was afraid that if he said anything Elsa would just tell him to screw off. Elsa shook her head and sighed. She bent over to lift her bag. Skinner felt himself start to get angry even though he didn't want to be. He put both hands on his hips like he was going to interrogate someone.

"So are ya?"

Elsa straightened up, cocked her head to the side and glared at Skinner.

"Am I what?!"

"Are you over at Luthorn College?"

"Well…what are you studying?"

Elsa put her bag back down and crossed her arms over her chest again.

"Geology. Geology, Officer Skinner."

Skinner's hands fell to his sides.

Elsa smiled.

"You remembered my name."

"Of course I remember your name. You helped put me in prison."

Skinner looked at his feet.

"I had to arrest you. After all of that evidence turned up that

■ ● ■

you killed your boyfriend, what was I supposed to do?"

"Gee… I don't know, Jerry. Maybe find out if I actually did the crime."

"Elsa, I did try, but the evidence just kept turning up."

Elsa turned her head. Skinner thought that she was staring off at a pool of bitter memories. He didn't want her to get stuck there.

Where are you headed for, Elsa? Maybe I could give you a lift?"

Elsa looked back at Skinner's face. He was smiling again.

"The Kent's farm. I'm heading out to the Kent farm."

Skinner grinned.

"Taxi'll cost you an arm and part of one leg. A stretch of road out there is still dirt and gravel. Let me give you a ride."

Elsa bent over, picked up her case and held it in both hands.

"You know what? Okay. But what's your boss going to say?"

Skinner chuckled.

"Not too observant today, are you? I'm the captain. You didn't notice?"

"Geee…was I that good for your career?"

Skinner took off his hat and tapped it lightly against his leg.

"If you stick around long enough, eventually everybody else leaves and then…"

"And then you get to be Captain."

Skinner tried to hide a sheepish smile by putting his hat back on slowly.

"Pretty much. My patrol car's over this way."

They walked to the car in silence. Skinner pulled his visor lower on his brow. Elsa raised a hand to her face to block the morning sun.

"I can throw that in the back seat."

"If you don't mind, I'll just keep this on my lap."

■ ● ■

Skinner opened the passenger door and held it for Elsa. Elsa stood by the door smirking at the officer.

"C'mon Jerry, I can get in a damn car by myself. No handcuffs, see?"

Elsa held up one hand and shook it.

"I'm not trying to be a jerk. Just trying to be polite."

Elsa turned away from him and then slowly turned back.

"I appreciate that Captain Skinner, but don't overdue it. I'm only here to visit the Kents and then I'm leaving."

"Yeah. Okay. I heard the Kent kid was home." Skinner closed the door as Elsa sat down and then ran to the driver's side and slid in. He started the engine, looked both ways and slowly pulled out. After five uncomfortable minutes Skinner felt like he had to start the conversation again.

"I heard the Kent kid was going up to see you at the prison. Course' he's not really a kid anymore."

Elsa turned her head toward Skinner.

"You seemed to have heard a lot of things, Jerry. Yes, he did. A few times."

"I guess he stopped. Did he know you that well?"

"Just from school."

Why'd he stop visiting?"

"Lots of time to follow up on gossip, huh Jer?"

Jerry looked left out his window. He glanced at Elsa and then his eyes went back to the road.

"Do you mind if I put my window down mon Capitan?"

"No. That's fine."

Jerry looked at his watch…9:28.

"Look, I'm sorry. But I guess I was really curious when I first heard he was going to see you. I suppose I'm being a jerk by trying to talk about this, but that always bothered me"

Elsa looked out her window trying to remember if the houses

■●■

they were passing or the landscape was really familiar or whether she was imagining that it was. She shook her head slightly and then glanced at Officer Skinner.

"No, you're fine. I don't mind talking about it that much actually."

Jerry stole a quick look at Elsa as he guided he car through a short series of small curves in the road.

"Well, why'd he stop going?"

"I told him not to come up anymore."

Jerry looked at Elsa again with a deep frown on his face.

"Watch the road, Captain Skinner."

"Yeah."

"One visit Kent came to me with this bullshit about how he could get me safely out of the prison, take me to Brazil and then we could live there together."

"What?!"

Elsa chuckled.

"Exactly. The second time he said this to me, and told me his plan couldn't fail, I told him to stay home. I said I'd refuse to see him if he ever came to the prison again."

"Was he serious?"

"Dead serious."

"Wow. I didn't realize he was crazy. He's in the city now, you know. But you probably already knew that."

"His mother let me know he was coming home to visit."

Elsa noticed that Skinner started frowning again.

"So you're going to what…thank him for not coming to see you any more' or thank him for his visits, even though he was crazy."

Elsa started laughing.

"I'm not so sure he was crazy. At least not about his plan. I'm convinced he thought he had a plan that he was sure was going

■ ● ■

to work. The part where we live together in Brazil is where it went bad"

Elsa looked out her window toward the horizon.

"Well it wouldn't have worked and you're out now and you're in college studying tectonic plates and exciting stuff."

Elsa burst out laughing again.

"Jerry, rocks. I study rocks. You're so damn sincere. You crack me up."

"Yeah, well…what made you decide to stuh-dee rocks? You must have found something exciting about it."

"C'mon Jerry. Why are you the Captain of a small town police force? Is it exciting?"

He looked out his side window. He twisted his neck a little to get some stiffness out.

"Satisfaction. I think it's satisfying to me."

Elsa folded her hands together on top of her case.

"That was a nice answer, Jerry. Very honest."

Elsa squeezed her hands together for a moment and then relaxed.

"Oh boy…when I was figuring things out in jail it just seemed like the thing to do. It was the thing I needed to do. I guess there was a drive in me that kind of developed. Some rocks are really hard to find. They're known, but most people don't get to see them. There were some rocks I really wanted to see. That's all."

"So it just hit you. Well, I'm glad you figured your stuff out."

"Oh, yeah. I figured a lot of stuff out."

"Uh huh…well, that's good, right?"

"Kind of came to me one day as I stood in the shower. I kind of felt like I was being watched by someone who wasn't there."

Skinner took a quick glance at Elsa and slowly shook his head.

■ ● ■

"I'm kind of surprised you said that. For some reason I didn't think you'd be someone who was spiritual."

"Oh no, no, no, no. I'm not. Jail drove that out of me completely. But I just started putting things together while I stood there naked in the shower. You know, being convicted and knowing you didn't do it…feeling…"

"But there was so much evidence, Elsa."

"So now we're going to argue? So much evidence. Good ol' Soup saw to that, didn't he?"

Skinner looked to his side.

"He's always been good at that detective stuff."

"Down right helpful. Good ol' Soup. Just kept coming up with piles of evidence. Amazing wasn't it?"

"Well, he kind of is."

"Of course he is. He's just amazing isn't he and this road needs some new gravel or you need to slow down so I don't bruise my brain on the roof of your paddy wagon."

"Sorry. Gets kind of rough out here after winter. Maybe you'll end up calling me a jack-ass for asking, but you're obviously very smart and you're one of the prettiest women I've ever seen around here and I wish you'd let me take you to dinner before you leave."

"You slut! I step off a train when you haven't seen me in ten years, and thirty minutes later, under cover of your badge, you try to intimidate me into going with you, somewhere, sometime, with some cop!! You give me a car ride and I'm supposed to be indebted to you enough to go out in public and let people see me drinking and eating with you? Who the hell do you think you are?! … Well?! Don't just sit there with your mouth hanging open! Apologize!"

"Intimidation? No…"

"This is a cop thing right? Try to get it on with a murderer?"

■ ● ■

"Wait a minute Elsa. I guess I had a bad idea. I don't sit at the train station waiting for single women to get off the train so I can impress them with my Smallville badge. I wasn't sitting there for the past ten years waiting for you to walk out on the platform, hoping you'd tell me all about Geology 101, or your prison memories. I'm glad you figured things out in jail and your life is straight. I got carried away and I shouldn't have and now I feel pretty stupid. I apologize, Elsa. I was out of line.

"Really? Stupid? Well from now on you refer to me as Ms. Landreth...God, that felt good! Unloading on you like that really felt good. Sorry. But I couldn't help myself."

Elsa giggled, tried to stop, but couldn't.

"Let's see how my visit with the Kents goes and maybe I'll take you up on that dinner.

Skinner did a double-take at Elsa and then turned left into a dirt driveway lined with flowers just breaking through the soil. Skinner stopped the car and sighed.

"Jesus Christ...okay... uhh, Ms. Landreth are you serious, or is this just you getting back at me still?" You beat me up like that and then agree to dinner?"

Skinner shook his head and sighed.

"Well let me see how my visit goes. I'll call for a cab back to town. Wow. Look at you. You are drenched in sweat. You sure you won't mind having dinner with a murderer, you being the police and all?"

"I'm not sure I believe that."

"Let's be serious for a second, Officer Skinner. You will be having dinner with a murderer. If you can handle that, in your position, how about we make it a definite and plan for seven? And will you have to be in uniform?"

Skinner laughed this time. He watched Elsa get out of the car and close the door. She leaned in through the open window.

■ ● ■

"Should I wear my dress uniform?

"Rather you didn't. Bad memories and all. You can bring your gun though."

Elsa started to stand.

"Hey…If you're not staying here tonight, what's with the suit case.?"

Elsa smiled.

"A rock sample.

"Rock sample?"

"Yeah. One I want to show Kent.

"Oooookay…so seven? Call the station and I'll pick you up….just one?"

"Yep. Just one."

Skinner started the engine and put the car in reverse."

"Well what's it called? Your sample?

"Kryptonite. Green Kryptonite."

■ ● ■

68

Inviolator

"C'mon. Let me at least go on some missions with you. I don't have to be a member, do I?"

"Do you really even have a superpower? I mean, you won't even talk about it."

"I'd rather show you what it is."

"That would be a good thing. Yeah. Like show me."

"I meant, on an evil-doer."

"A what?!"

"Don't laugh."

"I…I can't help it. 'An evil-doer?'"

Jonathan was so embarrassed he slid his hands into his pockets and he started looking at the ground. Sun-kiss stopped laughing, put her hands on her hips and shook her head.

"Look. You've got to show me something."

"I will. With an enemy. I can't just show you."

"I don't understand why not."

Jonathan raised his head and looked around. The man across the street glanced up and down the sidewalk, then jumped into a close-by alley.

Jonathan said, "Look."

■●■

Sun-kiss turned her head. "What...oh great! Did you have to point out the perve? Is that your power? Discovering perves who are jacking off in public?! I'm out of here."

Sun-kiss started off down the street.

Jonathan hollered, "Where are you going?"

"To get my bike."

He hollered again, "What kind? A Harley?"

"Why are you trying to have a conversation by hollering down the block at me?"

Jonathan felt stupid and ran after her to catch up.

"What kind of motorcycle do you have?"

Sun-kiss squinted at him and folded her arms.

"A bike. You know...as in bicycle. I ride a bicycle."

Jonathan was shocked. "You ride a bike to fight crime?"

"Well, whizzo, I don't have a car and paying for school is not cheap. Something wrong with riding a bike?"

"Uh, no. It's probably a really fast bike, but I have a car. I can give you a ride. Anywhere you want to go."

Sun-kiss dropped her hands to her side. "Uh-huh. Just because I went over the philosophy take-home with you doesn't mean we're friends. And it doesn't mean you get to tag along when I go on a mission. But I'll take a ride to Kent Lane."

"Deal. Let's go. My car is back this way."

Sun-kiss sneered. "Do you have enough gas?"

"Sure. Anywhere you need to go."

Under her breath Sun-kiss said, "You're just an innocent, aren't you?"

Jonathan turned around. "What?"

"Oh, nothing."

They walked two blocks to a parking lot. Jonathan unlocked the passenger side and went around to the driver's. Sun-kiss stared at the car and then at Jonathan over its roof.

■ ● ■

"You have an orange car."

"Yeah. Get in." Jonathan opened his door.

"You have a bright orange Datsun. How old is it? Does it still run?"

"Of course. Get in."

Sun-kiss shook her head hard and got in the car. She looked around the interior.

"You have a maid come in here to clean every Wednesday? It's God Damn spotless.

"I try to take care of it." Jonathan frowned. "I think I know where Kent Lane is, but could you remind me a little."

"We're heading for Corday. Then we make a right on Wayne. Corner of Kent and Wayne."

"That's out by the fields, isn't it? Got it."

"They drove in silence for ten minutes until Sun-kiss said, "Do you really have a superpower?"

Jonathan looked out his side window and then in the rear view mirror.

"Yes. I have a power."

"So then why won't you show me? I'm not going to let you just be Tag-a-long Boy."

Jonathan glanced at Sun-kiss, who was staring at him inquisitively.

"I guess I worry that you'll hate me, or find me repulsive."

"Oh, Jesus. You're not one of those guys who can stink, are you? Like Rancid?"

Jonathan laughed. "No."

"Because if you are, you can let me out right here and I'll walk the rest of the way."

"No. Nothing like that."

"Well, what…turn right here. It's four blocks down.

Jonathan made the right and stopped at a red light. "Well,

■ ● ■

when you were joining the League, how did you show your power? Was it like an exhibition or just an interview, or what?"

Sun-kiss started laughing.

"I just picked up a cup from the table, like this pretty one in your cup holder, and it heated up and…"

"Hey! It's melting !"

"Shit! I didn't think it was that kind of plastic. Damn it! It's all over. I'm so sorry."

Jonathan gave a weak, existential shrug. "That's okay, I guess. It was an accident, right? Maybe when it cools I can just peel it off the seats and floor."

"And the dashboard. Got some on the dashboard, too. I'm so sorry. At least it's a pretty color. Got anything else in here I can melt and make your car a real mess?"

Jonathan turned his head to glare at Sun-kiss. The light had changed and a car behind them was honking. Jonathan glanced in his rear view and muttered, "Darn it."

Sun-kiss mimicked him. "Darn it." Jonathan glared at her again. "I really am sorry. I'm embarrassed that I messed up the inside of your car. You take such good care of it. I'm really sorry. Hey! There's Hover-lad. Pull over."

Jonathan pulled his Datsun to the curb while Sun-kiss cranked her window down.

"Hey! Where are you going? I thought we had a meeting?"

"Evelyn, am I glad to see you. I'm heading to the hospital. Go-away Boy was shot."

"Shot? How could that be? Why didn't he just make somebody go away?"

"He did and they went. But then they shot him with a high powered rifle with a scope from about 100 yards away."

"Well, what happened to Mrs. McNulty? He was supposed to be guarding her and her formula."

■ ● ■

"He was, but They kidnapped her."

"They?"

"Yep. They kidnapped her. I wrote you a note inside." Hover-lad started to leave.

"Wait a minute! What happened?!"

Hover-lad moved back to the car. "I need to catch the trolley because the next one doesn't come for forty-five minutes."

"I could drive you."

Hover-lad bent down and stared at Jonathan. "Who's he, Evelyn?"

Sun-kiss glanced at Jonathan. "He's from my philosophy class."

"Oh…so I was coming back with lunch. Two guys had already been to the headquarters and Go-away Boy made them leave. They said they wanted to see Mrs. McNulty and he said 'no.' When I came back with lunch, the window by the refrigerator just shattered and Go-away fell on the floor bleeding. Mrs. McNulty started screaming and then someone was trying to break down the door to our HQ. I grabbed Mrs. McNulty and we climbed out the window by the bathroom. I tried to hover up to the roof with her, but she was too heavy. I could see someone running toward us across the fields with a rifle so we went back in the window. We tried to hide in the uniform closet behind Gigundo's costume. But Mrs. McNulty sneezed and they found us. One of them put a gun to my head and the other one dragged Mrs. McNulty out. The one with me backed out of the closet and yelled to his partner, 'What do we do with this one?' His partner said, 'shoot him.' When he had turned his head to ask his partner what to do, I hovered up to the air-conditioning duct and pulled myself in. Then I could hear him screaming, 'he turned himself invisible!' He was throwing costumes and stuff around and then he just started shooting. When he stopped his

■ ● ■

partner said, 'What in the hell are you shooting at? Let's get the hell out of here.' I pushed myself out of the AC and followed them out to their van. It's a white van that says 'Cockroach Extermination; They came and conquered.' I put my hover-hook on their bumper and hovered over their roof. They dragged me along behind them, but when they picked up speed out on 44 I rose too high and got tangled in the telephone lines and my fishing tackle broke. Then these crows started landing on the lines and started pecking at me. I managed to unhook my belt, and get away from those damn birds and get up high enough to see where the van was going. I can't remember the address right now, but I wrote it down inside on my note. Palettes's in the HQ. I got to go."

"Okay. Do you want Jonathan to give you a ride?"

"Nah. I can still catch the trolley." Hover-lad took off trotting toward the trolley stop.

"The HQ is two blocks up."

"That's what you call it? The HQ?"

Sun-kiss looked at Jonathan as they pulled up front of the building that served as the headquarters of the League of Individual Endows.

"Sometimes…just sometimes…" Sun-kiss whispered, "…we call it, the Headquarters." She smiled. "What the hell would you call it?"

"I don't know…the center…the lair…"

"Are you kidding me? The lair? Why the fuck would we call it 'The Lair?' Where do you get these ideas?"

"I don't know. I guess HQ works."

Sun-kiss got out of the car and slammed the door. Jonathan turned off the car and got out.

"Can I come in?"

Sun-kiss turned and stared at him. "Why not. C'mon."

■ ● ■

Sun-kiss pushed open the splintered door of the HQ.

"Gee, I thought you'd have a key pad or some other security thing."

"Geeee, we just have a good old-fashioned dead-bolt security thingy."

Palette came around the corner from the bathroom pulling up the zipper on his purple and yellow spandex body suit. He adjusted his goggles and looked up. "Sun-kiss! I'm so glad you're here."

"I'll bet. I'm actually surprised you're not gone already. But since you're here, let's dream up a plan to go get Mrs. McNulty and save her formula."

"Well, I do have to be somewhere else. Plus, I don't see how my power could be of any use in this situation.

Jonathan was shocked and felt confused. "Wait a second. Are you afraid?! I thought you were a member of the League. I've seen you in the newspaper. Your comrade is going into battle and you're leaving?!"

Palette stared at Jonathan with contempt. "Who the hell are you?!"

Sun-kiss started to reply, "He's with…"

"I'm the Inviolator."

It was quiet for ten seconds, then Sun-kiss turned around to face Jonathan with a smile on her face.

Palette's voice raised up to a squeaky falsetto, "The Inviolator? I've never heard of you."

"Oh…oh yeah? Well you probably don't want to know about me right now either. If you don't want to save Mrs. McNulty then just say so! Is it because the bad guys have guns and…"

"I don't have to listen to this. I've been on more missions than you'd be able to count. There's two of you. You should be able to handle this. I'm leaving!"

■ ● ■

Palette walked to the front door and stopped. He raised his goggles to his forehead and sent a 'snivering' smile toward Jonathan.

Jonathan frowned at him. "Bye-bye."

Palette left and Jonathan raised his hand to wave farewell. Jonathan's eyes almost exploded and he staggered backwards into a table. "They're green. My hands are green! What's wrong with me?! Did something happen to me?!"

"Stop the panic, Violation. That was Palette's parting gift. You're fine. Your face is green, too, by the way."

"What?!"

"Calm down. Palette changed your pallor, that's all. In four or five minutes you'll be back to normal…I hope."

"What?! Whad'ya mean, 'I hope?'"

"You'll be fine."

"Wait til I see that bastard again!"

"Why's that? Because Palette's never seen the unbridled rage of …of the Inviolator?" Sun-kiss started laughing. "Where the hell did you come up with that name from…Inviolator. I love it. You're a real pisser. And that little speech. 'Your comrade heading off into battle.' I loved that. That was cute." Sun-kiss picked up the note Hover-lad had written and began humming while she read. "You know, Palette's really a good guy. He's very smart. Working on a Phd in physics. But he is terrified of guns. If somebody has a gun, he is gone. If five guys have a one megaton neutron dirty bomb, he's all over it. He'll lead the charge… into battle." Sun-kiss shook her head and chuckled. "Weird guy, but nice."

"His power is color? He can change the color of things? That's his only power?"

Sun-kiss looked up at Jonathan. "Did you ever hear of someone with more than one power?"

■ ● ■

Jonathan felt stupid for the twentieth time that day. He shook his head, knowing that was a basic, fundamental truth. The super-endowed only had one power.

Sun-kiss went back to reading Hover-lad's note. "That would be something, though. A super-endowed with like two or three powers. That would be freaky. Okay, so I generally know where Mrs. McNulty is being held. You can drive over near there, drop me off and I'll see you in class for some Nicomachean ethics on Tuesday."

"What? You can't go alone. I'm going with you. These guys are dangerous."

"Uh-huh. And that's why I'm not going in there with a civilian slowing me down…Tag-a-long Boy. If you have a power, let's see it. Otherwise you're just Señor Chauffeur. And while we're at…oh shit…what the hell…oh God…" Sun-kiss slid her hand down the front of her jeans. "Turn around! Don't look at me! Turn the fuck arou…oh…damn.."

Jonathan turned his back on Sun-kiss. He saw the note she had been holding go fluttering past him and land on the floor. He felt Sun-kiss grab the top of his shoulder, tearing at his shirt. He started to turn around.

"What the…don't look at me!..keep your head tur…oh my God…oh…"

Jonathan heard Sun-kiss gasp and then her hand left his shoulder. Jonathan turned around as she sat down.

"What the hell?" She put a hand up to her forehead.

Jonathan looked at Sun-kiss. "So now maybe I can help?"

Evelyn dropped her hand and looked up at Jonathan. Her eyes got huge. "You?! What the…?! You did that? You son of a bitch. You did that?! That was you?! That's your power?! You make people masturbate?!"

"I know its kind of a weird power, but I think it could come

■●■

in handy."

"You?! You pull that shit on me again, ever, and I will burn your dick off. Do you understand me?"

Jonathan nodded solemnly. "So let's go get Mrs. McNulty."

Sun-kiss stood up, stepped toward Jonathan and pushed him in the chest with both hands, knocking him off balance. "Asshole."

"I'm sorry. How else could I show what I can do?"

"You could have just told me, dip shit."

"You would have told me to get out of your face."

"Hold the phone. That guy in the alley. Was that you, too?"

"Yeah. I thought you'd realize, but you didn't and I was embarrassed."

"Realize what? That your power is making people have auto-sex?! How far away can you influence someone to do that?"

"I'm not sure. Probably a couple of blocks. I never tried to find out. I can't just walk around making people get off on themselves on a sunny day somewhere downtown."

"Christ. Okay. Let's go get your car. But don't forget what I said."

"What?"

Jonathan's arm started to get uncomfortably warm. "Ow! Hey!"

"Don't forget."

"Yeah. Okay. Jesus."

Sun-kiss started toward the door.

"Hey. Don't you need to change into your uniform?"

Sun-kiss turned around with a smile on her face like one she had been saving to give to a two-year old. "Now why would I want to draw attention to myself…make myself a target. The uniform is for parades and charity events. Or going to the hospital to make sick kids feel happy."

■ ● ■

"Oh. Well why was Palette wearing his?"

"I told you he's weird. Plus he thinks it helps him pick up women. I can't imagine who the women are who go, "Oh my God! I've just got to get with that guy wearing the huge, bright red goggles with the dark blue lenses.' Must be the yellow and purple spandex, though I can't imagine that either. Anyway, can we go, now that our lesson in super-hero fashion is over?"

Jonathan picked up Hover-lad's note from the floor and handed it to Sun-kiss. "We'll need the address."

"I remember the address. It's a super-hero thing. Remembering addresses where 'evil-doers' hang out is important." She tossed the note on the table and headed for the door. Jonathan frowned and followed Sun-kiss out to his car.

"We're going to drive over to the park and get a horse drawn carriage to take us to the address."

"Why?"

Sun-kiss laughed. "Because your car is bright orange and it attracts attention even if someone is trying not to notice it."

"But won't a carriage?"

"Maybe. But we can slip out of a carriage and the carriage rolls away like there are still two people in it out for a ride."

Jonathan steered the car toward the park and had to stop twice for trolleys going in opposite directions. "Why don't we take a trolley and just walk over?"

Sun-kiss stared at Jonathan. "Just drive to the park."

Jonathan parked his car across from the carriage stand. Sun-kiss got out and went over to the first carriage in line. She spoke with the driver and pulled money out of her pocket to count. As Jonathan crossed the street Sun-kiss turned around with her eyebrows raised. "You got any money? I'm $2.42 short."

"Well how much is it?"

"Twenty bucks."

■ ● ■

"I've got it."

"You've got it? You shouldn't have to pay. This is your first mission. Nobody pays on their first mission."

"Well don't tell anybody."

Jonathan handed the driver a twenty and they both climbed into the carriage. The driver turned around and looked at each of them.

"Aren't ya' one of those super-endows? I've seen ya' in the newspaper, haven't I?" Pointing at Sun-kiss, "You made the honorary first pass at the Lacrosse Championships, right?"

Jonathan said sarcastically, "She sure did. This is Sun-burn."

The driver smiled. "And who are you to be with such an important lady?"

"Me? Nobody. I'm just taking a ride."

"He's kidding. This is Violin. Don't get him started or he'll whine and whine you into a coma."

The driver said, "Auditory power, huh?"

Jonathan glared at Sun-kiss through her smirk. "Can we get going now? Sun-burn is on a mission. Ow!"

"Keep it up, Violetta. I'll give you a sun burn you'll never forget."

The driver turned back to his horses. Over his shoulder he said, "Golly. You should'a said somethin'. If I'da known you two were on a mission I would'na sat here chattin' with ya'.

Sun-kiss gave the driver the address as the carriage moved off. Fifteen minutes later Sun-kiss told the driver to angle his carriage toward a small stand of trees and a hedge.

"Jonathan…when we get near the hedge we get out on your side and walk along with the carriage. When we get to the corner of the building we sprint toward those trees. Got it?"

Jonathan nodded.

"Little nervous?"

■ ● ■

Jonathan nodded again.

The driver said, "I'm gonna slow down here just a little. Good luck."

"Thanks. Step out, Jonathan."

Jonathan jumped down from the carriage followed by Sun-kiss. They walked alongside for ten paces, then Sun-kiss grabbed Jonathan's arm and they ran for the side of the building. From the hedges they watched the carriage disappear around the next corner.

"Come on, Mr. Inviolator. We're going through the front door."

They stuck close to the façade of the building and then slipped through the open front door. Ahead of them was a concrete staircase. On each side of the staircase were two slightly opened doors.

"Let's get up there. No noise."

"Wait. How do we know she's not down here?"

"Because evil-doers always go up the second or third floor so they can see whoever comes to rescue somebody. Now let's go and no noise."

They went half way up the stairs when an empty Cremey Crème Mint soda can went clanging to the bottom of the staircase and banged against the wall. They both stood still watching until it stopped spinning. Sun-kiss growled, "I guess we should have called first. One God Damn soda can on these stairs and you find it with your foot! What the hell, Jonathan?!"

"You think they heard us?"

"Nah. They're probably three-fourths deaf and listening to ZZ Top full tilt with head phones on." Sun-kiss looked up the stairs again and sighed. "Let's go."

They climbed to the first landing and began to open a door. It slammed open knocking Sun-kiss backwards into Jonathan.

■ ● ■

He grabbed the railing and Sun-kiss so that they wouldn't fall down the stairs. Jonathan looked to his left. A man with a shotgun had come down from the third floor and was pointing it at them. The man from the door had a pistol against Evelyn's neck.

"You both come in here and sit down."

Jonathan and Sun-kiss did as they were told.

Jonathan whispered, "Why didn't you burn them?"

"I can only do one thing at a time. Want to get shot?"

"Shut up! Both of you. Pete, grab that extra rope from the closet."

"You think they're endows, Jackie?"

"I don't know. They haven't done anything but make a lot of noise so far." Jonathan clasped his hands in his lap and looked down at them feeling incredibly stupid. Five minutes later they were both securely tied to their chairs.

Jonathan looked up at Jackie. "Where's Mrs. McNulty?"

Jackie looked at Pete and then back at Jonathan. "Like you're going to do what?"

"If They hurt her, you'll pay the ultimate fine for it." Jackie, Pete and Sun-kiss all stared at Jonathan. Jackie chuckled. Pete laughed. Sun-kiss giggled. Jonathan snapped his head toward her. She looked down and whispered, "Sorry."

"Uh-huh. So who the hell are you, kid?"

"I'm…I'm the Inviolator."

Jackie struggled to keep a straight face. "Really. I didn't know that. And who are you? You look familiar."

"I'm nobody. I'm just along for the ride."

"An endow groupie. With Violation, here? That's hard to believe. Someone who…hey…what's that smell? Something's burning. You smell it, Pete?"

"Yeah. What the…damn…oh damn…fuck.."

Jackie jumped up out of his chair and backed away from

■ ● ■

Pete.

"Put your dick back in your pants. Stop it! Get the hell away from me, you pervert. You trying to put on a show for our captives?! Don't point that thing at me, God Damn it!"

"Can't…can't help it…can't…oh shit…"

"Go to the bathroom! What the hell is wrong with you?!"

Pete stumbled toward a door, slammed into it and fell down. He awkwardly stood back up and shuffled through the bathroom door.

"Ow!" Jonathan glared at Sun-kiss.

"Shut up, kid!"

"You shut up, pinhead."

"Why you stupid little breen."

Jackie rose from his chair and moved toward Jonathan. When he was ten feet away he dropped his gun, grabbed his wrist and screamed. He became wide-eyed, then slipped one hand down the front of his pants. Jonathan strained at the burning ropes and they snapped. He jumped up and lunged for Jackie's gun just as the shotgun blasted over his head.

Sun-kiss screamed, "Run!"

They flew through the door, leap-frogged steps two and three at a time. When they got to the sidewalk Sun-kiss hollered, "Run for the park." She veered off through a stand of trees as the first pistol shots tore bark off the trees ahead of them.

Panting, as he ran harder than he'd ever run before, he tried to say to Sun-kiss, "You…you can only do…ten or fifteen feet."

"Yehs."

"Shoulda…should told me."

"Run."

Jonathan looked over his shoulder. Pete slowed down a little and Jonathan could see he had his penis in his hand, but he was still shooting and still coming. Jackie passed Pete, but now he

■ ● ■

had one hand in his pants and was stumbling.

"I…I influenced both…both of them."

"Yeah…but…but they're still shootin'."

"But they're…missing. That's…good…right?"

They made it to the park just as a trolley passed in front of them.

"Veer away from the trolley so no civilians get hit." Bullets started sailing all around them. Men and women on the trolley screamed and hollered. Sun-kiss yelled, "Head for the Ice House." They sprinted to the Ice House and pushed past the ticket-taker.

Jonathan screamed, "Run! They have a bomb in the building!" The fifteen skaters went into a short moment of paralysis and then ran for the exits. Alarms went off as people pounded through the emergency doors.

"Now what?"

Sun-kiss ignored Jonathan and walked out to the center of the skating rink.

"They'll be coming through those doors any second now. What…"

In seconds Jonathan could barely make out Evelyn's image through the steam. Jonathan slid his feet across the quickly melting ice to the edge of the rink. He heard the doors slam open over by the entrance.

"Over here, pinhead." Three shots came in his direction in rapid succession. Jonathan ran along the edge of the rink holding the rail, and yelled again. They must be desperate to recruit vicious, vapid fools like you to their organization." Jonathan could hear them splashing through the water toward him. 'Now,' he thought. He heard Jackie start cursing. Pete was yelling "what's wrong with me?!" And then there was a splash followed by a second one.

■ ● ■

"I lost my gun."

There were two more random shots and, "Shit! I'm out…oh fucking damn it…oh shit…out'a …shit…bullets…God damn!"

Jonathan slid across the ice toward where he heard their voices. He found one gun and saw it wasn't empty. "Sun-kiss! I have them covered!" Then he heard something he hadn't expected.

"Son of a bitch! I'm gonna burn your dick off."

"Oh hell…Damn, Sun-kiss. I didn't know you were close to them. I didn't do it on purpose. Really. You just got in the way of my influence."

The steam was thinning out and there were sirens blaring all around the building. The They agents were arrested and dragged away. Sun-kiss and Jonathan made their way back to the HQ after being thanked for their services by a police captain. The newspaper photographers kept taking their pictures all the way to Jonathan's car. Gigundo had read the note Hover-lad left and followed them to the They building and found Mrs. McNulty. Gigundo, Sun-kiss and Jonathan sat around a table in the HQ catching each other up on their parts in the rescue.

"Why don't you guys put some posters up on the walls or something? Everything is just grey-green in here."

Gigundo frowned at Jonathan. "Who are you again? I understand you helped Sun-kiss on her mission, but who are you?"

"I'm Jonathan and I…"

Sun-kiss glanced at Jonathan and interrupted him. "He's the Inviolator. Uhhh, he makes people fall down."

Gigundo's eyebrows raised up. "Cool. I'd like to see that some time. Great name. But right now, I gotta go to work. I'm on second shift tonight." Gigundo walked out of the meeting room and stopped at the splintered door. "I'll borrow some of my father's tools tomorrow and fix this door. See ya."

"Did I just see him shrink?"

■ ● ■

"Christ, you thought he'd be that pudgy all the time?"

"Pudgy?! He's huge!"

"And I'm still pissed at you. Don't you ever tell them what happened in the Ice House." She stared at Jonathan with red, glowing eyes.

"Don't do that, Evelyn. That's a little too freaky. I couldn't even see you in the steam. I swear I didn't know you were there."

"Uh-huh...I almost bit through my tongue, afraid Pete and Jackie would hear me and figure out where I was, you bastard."

Tuesday morning Jonathan entered the lecture hall and looked around. He saw Sun-kiss sitting over to his right and wandered over.

"Hey."

"Hey."

"Is it alright if I sit here?"

Sun-kiss looked up at him. "Sure. It's a free lecture hall...I guess."

The lecture hall filled up and the professor walked down the aisle to the podium. When he turned around the room grew quiet.

"Ow!" Jonathan jumped up rubbing his butt.

From the front of the lecture hall Jonathan heard, "You have a pressing question?"

"No, sir. No, I apologize." Jonathan sat back down and saw that Sun-kiss had a huge smirk on her face. He whispered, "What the hell did you do that for?"

"Just don't forget. One more time and your dick is fried bacon."

Jonathan sat up straight, glowering at Sun-kiss. Then he leaned toward her ear. "There are 150 students in here. If you get off on yourself in here you will never, ever live it down on this campus. So can we have a truce?"

■ ● ■

Sun-kiss looked around the full lecture hall thinking about her reputation and two more years of school. "Sure."

Jonathan leaned toward Sun-kiss again. "I keep forgetting to ask. Did you know what Mrs. McNulty's formula was for?"

"Sure…chocolate chip cookies."

"What?!" Jonathan was loud enough to catch the attention of the professor and half of the lecture hall.

"Young man, if you are intent upon interrupting my lecture for some obscure political reason, I suggest you go out into the hall and play kowtow to your whimsy out there."

From somewhere behind them a student commented, "He's that Inviolator dude. I saw his picture in the paper."

Slowly comments started building all around them about Jonathan being the Inviolator. One female student leaned over Evelyn's shoulder and asked for an autograph. Jonathan started to reach for the pen and paper when his thigh started to get very warm.

"No. I'm sorry. The members of the League don't do autographs. I'm sorry."

"Well, here. Take this and call me later."

Jonathan looked down at the phone number, watched the paper slowly turn a burnt brown and then crumble.

The professor brought order back to the class.

Jonathan brushed the burnt paper onto the floor. He whispered, "Chocolate chip cookies?"

"Lot's of money in cookies. Say, can I have a ride to HQ after class? Someone stole my bike."

■●■

The Suit

When I decided to become a writer there were certain things I fully expected to happen. Of course I knew there would be rejections. There'd be pats on the back by people who thought my writing was crap but wouldn't say so. I anticipated that there would be people who would say I needed to learn the rules of writing. They would cite Chekhov and I would lean on Hemingway.

I knew that I would eventually pass through at least one writing group where the participants didn't do much writing, but would have a lot to say about what I was writing. Even so, I supposed that any type of feedback would be helpful.

So I was writing and I had a couple of pieces published. I had thought that if I worked hard enough, maybe something good would come of it. What 'good' was, I wasn't quite sure.

What I didn't expect was the letter. I can still clearly remember how I felt when I scanned it the first two times sitting at my kitchen table. The third time I rose from my chair and started pacing. Then I started laughing while I paced. This had to be a joke and I started wondering which of my friends would be most likely to try to play it out.

■ ● ■

I called Alan, who immediately started laughing but denied having anything to do with the letter. When he regained his composure, he said he thought it didn't sound like a joke. Just that quickly my pacing speeded up. "You might want to run it by someone in the legal world to see if it's legit or bullshit. Probably even a legal aide would be able to give you an idea."

I felt like I was panicking. "Alan, I don't have a lawyer. I don't know where to start."

"Okay dude, don't go over the edge, I have a friend named Connor who's a lawyer. Let me give him a ring and I'll get right back to you."

So while Alan reached out to his friend I began pacing in my kitchen in a circle, stopping at my refrigerator to see what I didn't have in it but thought maybe I should. I was being sued for $90,000 for stealing a story from someone I'd never heard of and was certain I didn't know. The letter said I had stopped someone from turning his story into a movie and deprived him of substantial rewards from his work and efforts.

Who was this guy? I started thinking I should get on the internet to find out who this guy was who was trying to shake me down. That's what it was. A shake down.

The phone rang. "Hello. My name is Connor Blake. May I please speak with Hollis Carey. We have a mutual friend named Alan Sellers and he asked me to give you a call."

He listened to me explain my problem, asked me to come to his office the following morning and confirmed that I was actually being sued.

Whoever this guy was, he was suing me over a short story I had posted on my website. I called it "The Day Before We Left". As far as I could tell no one else had published or posted anything close to that title or content. From my inexpert, ignorant reading of the notice, it was being claimed I had infringed on

■ ● ■

'someone's ability to make money from a story I had supposedly stolen from 'someone'. Who the hell was 'someone'?

At 9:00a.m. the next day I sat down in Connor Blake's small office with peach colored walls and a framed poster of Huey Newton and Bobby Seale. I had expected piles of files all over the room. Instead, on one wall from floor to ceiling was a book-case of law tomes. Against the other wall was an eight foot long table with neatly stacked files covering it. Connor had extended his hand first and I saw that he was in a wheelchair.

"My partner, Kareem Lewis, is very good at this type of work. His doctoral thesis was on the 'Berne Convention for the protection of Literary Work…'or something like that. So if you don't mind I'll read this over and we'll wait for Kareem to show up." I was thinking, 'oh great, so I'll be hanging for the next two hours waiting for the partner to show'.

"Are you sure your partner will be here soon. I have to be at work by noon."

"He's rarely late…and what kind of work do you do for your day gig?"

"I work in an auto parts shop."

"Are you handy with cars?'

"I'm not a top mechanic, but I keep my own car going."

"Depending upon what we may be getting into, would you be willing to do some car repair or maintenance in exchange for legal work?"

"You mean barter?"

"Essentially."

"So this is real. Do you think this is going to be involved?"

"Yes, it's real. Good morning, Kareem. This is Hollis Carey. He's a friend of my pal Alan."

We shook hands and Kareem's eyes immediately began scan-

■●■

ning the paper Connor handed him. I began scanning the partners. Kareem had dreads that went half-way down his back. He wore a dark blue suit, white shirt, and a brilliant blue tie. Connor had light brown, almost blond hair parted on one side that just hit his shoulders. He was wearing a light blue button-down oxford shirt. For some reason I assumed he was wearing jeans.

"What do you think, Kareem?"

"Shouldn't be a big problem to resolve," Kareem smiled at me, "Unless you actually physically stole his story." He smiled again and Connor chuckled.

"No. I didn't steal his story in any form and I did a poor man's copyright."

"You posted the story on your website?"

"Yes."

"The time stamp on the post should be good enough for us."

"You ever meet this Charles Filet?"

"No."

"Maybe at a writer's conference?"

"I'm sure I haven't."

"Have you been to Canada recently?"

"Yeah. Twenty years ago with my Mom and Dad."

"I'll give Monsieur Filet's solicitor a call and see how we can get this straightened out.

I nodded.

"Kareem…how's your car running?

"Needs an oil change but basically okay. Why, does someone need a ride?"

"Mr. Carey will be trading automotive work for legal help and counseling."

Kareem stared at me and then said "Okay. Connor, I have to be down to Escort Street to interview a client so I have to go."

"Okay. I have McGary coming back this afternoon. Mr.

■ ● ■

Carey, it's been interesting meeting you and we'll be in touch about the suit and the oil change."

I shook hands with both of them and headed for work.

I was receiving letters from Charles Filet's lawyers twice a week now. They were starting to get on my nerves even though Kareem said there was not much to worry about. I figured this might go on forever or until the people who wanted to buy the film rights got tired and went away. In two weeks I had done one oil change and cleaned the headlights on Connor's car, so I didn't feel I was being taken advantage of.

But I went to the office one day because Connor had received a letter proposing a settlement. When I walked into the office I heard Kareem say "fuck that!!" I sat down in front of Connor's desk. Behind me from Kareem's office I heard him say" I'm going to drive up to Montréal on Friday. These pissants won't return my calls. They don't address my enquiries, I'm going to go up and confront these ass-jockeys face to face!"

"Pissants, huh? Connor started laughing.

I looked at Kareem over my shoulder. "What's an ass jockey?" Kareem looked embarrassed. "I don't know.

Kareem went to Canada and came back and said they wouldn't show him Filet's story because they said you had already stolen it. Then he was kicked out of their office because he hadn't made an appointment and they had to go to an important meeting. Kareem said we may have to engage a barrister in Montréal if we want to end the harassment.

The knock on the door on a Wednesday was just a knock on the door on a Wednesday. I opened the door to three men in suits. The youngest one held out a wallet holding a police badge.

■ ● ■

I said, "Yes? How can I help you?"

One of the two older men said, "Nous sommes de la police de Montréal et nous devons vous poser quelques questions."

"I'm sorry. I don't speak French."

The younger guy with the American badge said, "These men are detectives from Canada. They want to talk with you about a murder."

"A murder? What murder?"

The other older man was holding out a badge that apparently said he was with the police in Montréal. "Est-ce que vous connaissez Charles Filet?"

"Look, I'm sorry. I don't speak French."

"Well you probably want to talk to them considering the position you are in."

"What position?! What the hell are you talking about?"

The young American cop stared at me like he thought I would get weak-kneed and fall down from his glare.

"What are you?! The translator?"

One of the two Canadians said, "Sir…there's no need for a translator. But if you please just spare us a few minutes of your time. We are trying to gather information on the murder of Charles Filet. We will only take a few moments."

When I heard Filet's name again my curiosity went to eleven. I heard my voice in a tunnel say, "Please come in. We can sit at my kitchen table." Did they think I had something to do with it?

As we sat down the two Canadians took out notebooks. The American wandered over to the kitchen window and started looking down into the street.

"Est-ce que vous connaissez Charles Filet?"

"Look, I'm sorry. I don't speak French."

"How well did you know Charles Filet?

■ ● ■

"I didn't know him at all."

"Correspondence with your name on it was found in his apartment."

"Probably from my lawyer."

"What is your lawyer's name?'

"Let me call my lawyer and maybe he can come over here."

"There's no need for that."

"In your situation you would probably do yourself a favor by being more open." The American cop was a jerk and was working hard to prove it.

I went through my wallet and came up with Connor's business card and while I was handing it over I watched the American stroll over to a shelf that I had notebooks on. He began perusing them and I completely missed a question one of the Canadians asked.

"What the fuck do you think you are doing?"

One of the Canadians looked over his shoulder and started shaking his head.

The young cop turned to me and with a sneer said, "I think you need to concentrate on the interview and not worry about me."

"Oh, really? Well, you need to concentrate on walking out my door."

He turned away from me.

"Don't' act like you didn't hear me. Get out. Get the fuck out."

"I'll leave when your interview is over."

"Oh, yeah? You didn't notice the interview just ended about thirty seconds ago?! Gentlemen, I'm sorry. I will have to contact my lawyer. I'm not going to be answering any questions until I see my lawyer, so you'll have to leave."

"Nous sommes désolés."

■ ● ■

As they left, I wished this had gone differently. I really wanted to know what happened to Filet. They left calmly but I thought the Canadians looked disappointed. One of them was shaking his head slightly.

I called Connor to tell him what had happened. He wanted me to come to his office immediately. When I walked into the office, I heard Kareem say, "He was sure they mentioned murder?"

"At least that's what Hollis said.

"Does Hollis speak French?"

As I sat down I said "No, Hollis does not speak French."

At first it bothered me that Kareem sounded so exceedingly calm.

After I thought a little it occurred to me that I should want a lawyer who was calm and logical. Apparently I was being accused of murder.

"You say those cops from Montréal kept speaking French to you. Can you guess why?"

"I don't know. Maybe because they speak French every day in Montréal. How's that for a 'why'? Are you thinking they're trying to trip me up somehow?"

"I think it's weird that after you told them you didn't speak French that they kept trying their French on you.

"You said you haven't been in Canada in about twenty years?"

"That's right. The last time I was there I was in Hamilton."

"Is that where the cops found the body?"

"I guess so. I was having a hard time concentrating. I was watching the American cop wander around my apartment looking at stuff."

"Did they tell you they found the body in Hamilton in English or French?"

"C'mon. Really?" If they told me in French I wouldn't know

■ ● ■

what they said. Am I under suspicion? Your questions are start-ing to sound a little less than sympathetic."

"Just trying to get a grip on why the Canadian authorities would send two cops from Montréal down here…kind of an odd situation don't you think?"

"Having never been accused of murder before, I'd say 'yes' except I have no idea what it's like when you get a normal accu-sation of murder dropped on you."

Connor finally interjected with, "Actually no one has accused you of murder, but that could change in the next twenty-five seconds or so."

The outer door opened and the three detectives walked into the office. I looked at Connor and said, "The boy has to go."

The young American clearly didn't like my comment.

His face flushed red and he said, "I ain't going nowhere. Your lawyers are here and now you can start answering some ques-tions here or we can take a trip down to our station. What's convenient for you?"

"I hate to disappoint your arrogant ass, but we don't answer anything if you are in here." Kareem looked pissed. To the Cana-dians he said, "We may be willing to talk with you two, but you'll have to ask sideshow to wait in the car. Understand?"

One of the Canadians whispered "sideshow"? The other one said something in French and they both smiled. The older of the two Canadians spoke to the American. "We would like to get this interview over as easily as possible, so could you please wait for us outside? This shouldn't take very long."

The American was visibly stung but he turned and left the office. It just didn't appear to be his day.

Kareem went into his office and pulled a couple of chairs and angled them into Connor's office somehow. Connor tapped my arm and put his index finger up to his lips. Clearly I wasn't to

■ ● ■

speak.

Kareem sat the two Canadians down and then said, "Officers, why have you come here?"

We are investigating the murder of Charles Filet. Mr. Carey seems to have had some type of relationship with M. Filet. His name was mentioned on documents we found in Filet's office."

"Mr. Filet was bringing a suit against Mr. Carey, so his name would naturally appear in correspondence." Both Canadians were nodding their heads.

"So you know that. So then why are you here? What else do you have?"

"We have M. Filet's diary."

Connor started tapping one finger on his desk. "Uh huh... And?"

"In it he wrote that he was becoming increasingly frightened of Mr. Carey." From my angle it appeared that Kareem was surprised.

Connor said evenly, 'Our client hasn't been in Canada in twenty years."

"We are aware he is claiming that. His last visit was to Hamilton. Filet's body was found in Hamilton. We have no reason at this time to believe that Mr. Carey may have slipped across the border while riding with someone else."

"So now we're in a conspiracy to murder?"

"Not necessarily. Maybe he was simply taking a ride with someone across the border."

"I didn't take any ride across any border!"

Connor grabbed my arm.

Kareem smiled." Do you have anything that would suggest that Mr. Carey has been in Montréal or Hamilton or any other Canadian city?

"No. but we have a photo of you visiting M. Filet's solicitor

■ ● ■

at his office. Perhaps Mr. Carey was close by.

Kareem's smile disappeared and a frown took over. Connor asked to see the photo. "Kareem, you may want to get a copy and have it framed. It's pretty good, but it's not from a street camera is it? So what the hell was going on at the office where Filet had his legal work done?!"

"What do you mean?"

"Connerie! You know exactly what I mean. So on a random day, when you couldn't possibly know that Mr. Lewis was going to see Monsieur Filet's solicitor, you manage to come up with a professional looking photo when he goes inside for less than half an hour. You were looking for something that was going on there and then you dump all of this information that you probably wouldn't expose in any other investigation."

The Canadians just stared.

"Okay. If it's like that …just get out. Sortez! When you want to explain what's going on, come back."

The Canadians left without saying a word.

The three of us were silent for a good moment or two.

"Kareem, you have any thoughts on what's going on up there?

"Connor, I am a blank. I don't know what Hollis has been doing but I don't want to have any part of it."

I couldn't help myself. I immediately stood up. And then heard Connor laughing, so I sat back down, slightly embarrassed.

"That wasn't funny."

"Of course not…but then again"…Kareem grinned.

Connor and Kareem both started laughing.

I drove home, slowly pondering that somehow I'd gotten involved in some kind of international murder conspiracy. 'Come on Hollis…You're not in some kind of spy movie or story. Probably just some drug thing. All I did was write a story that someone liked or thought was close enough to Filet's that…that what? I don't even know. Where the hell am I?! Did I really just miss my turn?'

I climbed the stairs to my second floor apartment listening to voices I never heard before. Mainly because I don't hang out with cops much. The Canadians were standing in the hallway leaning against the wall. When they noticed me they began walking toward me.

"Mr. Carey, This was not our idea."

"We are very sorry. This is inappropriate."

"We apologize."

I stared at them and realized my apartment door was open. "How'd you get in my place?! What's going on?"

"Everything was already occurring when we arrived."

I pushed past the two detectives and went to the entrance to my apartment and was 'greeted' by a police officer who put his hand on my chest to stop me from going in.

"What's going on? I live here!"

The young American cop approached me with a sneer shining from his very even teeth.

"This is called a search warrant. We are executing a search." He handed me the paperwork and walked away. Policemen were going through my notebooks. Two policemen were in my bedroom.

"Sir? Could you step out here a second?" I walked out into the hall and one of the Canadians said, "We called your lawyers immediately when we found out what was going to happen."

As soon as he finished speaking I saw Kareem come through the downstairs door pushing a wheelchair. I slipped down the

■ ● ■

stairs quickly to help Kareem bring Connor up.

When we got upstairs Kareem took the warrant from my hand. Suddenly Kareem yelled "The warrant doesn't cover those closets so get the hell out of there!" The young cop walked over and started arguing with Kareem.

"Sorry we didn't get here earlier. Those Canadian cops called us and as soon as I tracked down Kareem we came here."

"Thanks, Connor. How concerned should I be about this? I mean these guys could plant anything."

"I doubt you have to worry about that. I don't think our Canadian friends would accept that."

"You mean you think Canadian cops are more pure or something?"

"No. I think these two want a clean bust."

"So why are they standing in the hallway?"

"Probably worried about not compromising the warrant. You can't bring the whole ballpark in with you when you execute a search warrant.

Kareem approached us frowning. "This is some bullshit. The cop over there who applied for the warrant is Sgt. Douglas. The judge who granted the warrant is Judge Douglas."

Two hours later and a lot of arguing with raised voices, the cops left with copies of the letters Filet's solicitor's had sent me and three notebooks. We were given a list of what the cops were taking and then it was over.

While Connor, Kareem and I finished off a six pack, Alan called to see how the suit was coming." You mean the one where I'm being investigated for murder? Talk later, Alan."

As I was hanging up we could all hear Alan yelling "Hey!! Hey! Hollis...hollis." We all had smiles radiating over the kitchen table.

■ ● ■

Nothing happened for a couple of days and then Connor called me and asked if I could come to the office. When I walked in the Canadians were sitting in front of Connor's desk. Kareem was leaning in the doorway. Connor told me to have a seat. I said I'd rather stand.

"We have come to apologize, we are sorry for any tension this situation has caused you. We have arrested the murderer of Charles Filet. He was trying to get the story Filet had written because he heard that someone was trying to buy the film rights for a lot of money. But the film group came across your story and they were afraid they would not have exclusive control of the story because your piece was so similar to Filet's story. Filet said in his diary that he became increasingly terrified of you, but you don't have a photo of yourself on your website so apparently the murderer pretended to be you.

"What about the jerk cop who turned my apartment upside down?"

"We can't really apologize for 'sideshow'. He is young and apparently very stupid with influential relatives. We will be leaving and thank you for your time. The last thing, we were hoping that you would not rewrite the story to make us seem as foolish as our young American counterpart."

"Naw. I'll keep the story basically the same. Okay?"

Both Canadians smiled at me and then left, supposedly heading for Montréal.

A few days later there was a knock on my door. A man in sunglasses said "Are you Hollis Carey?" I looked at the two men shifting back and forth.

"ummmm…who are you?"

We read a story of yours on the internet. We are interested in discussing the purchase of your film rights from you. Can we

■ ● ■

come in?"

"No. my girlfriend is dressing."

I closed the door, went to the phone and called Connor.

"Don't let them in and call the police."

"Connor, they're coming through the door as we speak. Call for me.

■ ● ■

Aficionado

They say even a broken clock is right twice a day. Not this one. The clock here says two o'clock. But a freight train comes through at about 1:55 every day and the walls in the diner start to vibrate. And while the coffee cups clink, the minute hand on the clock slips to 2:05and then slowly to 2:10. And finally the minute hand releases its grip on 2:10 and it glides around the clock's circumference until it hits two o'clock again. By then the train is gone. So maybe the clock is right once a night, but I wouldn't know. I'm never here then. If I'm lucky, I'm home in bed wrapped up in dream skein of red Chinese silk, unbruised, with Louise lying next to me.

The waitress is still standing under that broken clock at the other end of the counter. Her hands are still in the register till and I still want to kill her. She's ignored me for at least an hour, I think. Maybe it hasn't been that long, but it sure feels that way. I asked her for another cup of coffee and she said, "Don't bother me, I'm countin." That was half an hour ago. How much could there be in that register to count? Maybe she's really bad at math.

And the damn author. How long's he going to keep me wait-

∎●∎

ing for him? I don't even know what he wants.

Funny. The day looks sunny now. A little half turn ago on the stool and the sky was completely gray…Stray pieces of newspaper were flying by the windows. I was watching them get snapped up in the air and then flutter back down. Probably from the obituaries. Now it's completely sunny and calm. It's almost like someone can't make up their mind about what the weather should be like.

"You want anything else?"

I'm not a jumpy guy, but the waitress's screechy voice made me scrunch my shoulders like I expected a nun to cuff me in the back of my head. I think I grimaced when I spun around. I would have sworn the waitress was twenty years younger than the person I was looking at now. I tilted my head a little to look for the other waitress. I guess I haven't been paying enough attention to my surroundings.

"Ya lookin' for pie or sumthin'? Ain't got any. All out."

"Okay. How about a tea?"

She actually sneered at me and then squinted her eyes.

"A tea…" She said it so condescendingly I got pissed off.

"Yeah! A goddam tea. The coffee you served me an hour ago tasted like paper."

"What ya' expect in a place like this?! Yer in here enough to know what the coffee tastes like. And you only been in here shy of ten minutes, Mr. Chronomaniac."

She walked away muttering, "Hour my ass."

I was primed to curse her out, but the "ten minutes" threw me. "I've only been in here ten minutes?!"

She looked at me like I had my elbow in the catsup. "Yer' watch stop?"

Without taking my eyes off her I dropped my hands below the counter and rubbed my left wrist. No watch. Didn't I have a

■ ● ■

watch when I left the apartment this morning? 'Chronomaniac.' Where the hell did she get that from?

Finally. The author is coming through the revolving door. If this has been ten minutes, it was the longest ten minutes of my life. From behind me, in a sing-song voice, I heard, "Hi! Can I get you anything?" The waitress has suddenly gone flirtatious. And what the hell is with her face? She looks like she's in her thirties, now that she's beaming at the author and he's beaming back at her.

I can't believe this. I'm getting pissed. "I'm almost sorry to interrupt, and how long were you going to keep me here chilling my butt on this diner stool with the chameleon in curlers?"

The waitress seemed outraged. I almost laughed. "I never come in here in curlers!

"Sorry, it's laundry day for me and I had to put my clothes in the dryer."

"So I gotta sit here waiting for you a goddam hour while you screw around with your dirty laundry?" He looked genuinely confused.

"Was it that long? He glanced at the waitress.

"Nah. By my watch, twelve minutes."

He smiled. She smiled. I frowned. When the heck did she put that red lipstick on?

She pushed her hair away from her face. Is that my watch?! I shook my head.

"Look…can you and I get down to business…whatever that is."

The author gave an almost imperceptible nod to the waitress and she drifted off to the other end of the counter and stood under the broken wall clock. She gave us a glance and then picked up a rag and started trying to rub a hole through the formica counter top.

■ ● ■

I turned back to the author and found him staring at pieces of newspaper floating past the windows in slow motion.

I shook my head and cleared my throat. He turned his head toward me with a blank expression. He gave me the impression having been hypnotized.

"So why are we here?"

He smiled and looked down at the floor. "I need you to find someone. I need you to find the person who killed Angela Scott."

I shivered. Something felt definitely wrong.

He handed me a newspaper article about a woman who was killed three years before and the crime was never legally solved. There was a suspect who sued the Telegraph successfully for suggesting that he was the solution to the crime without presenting any evidence. The Telegraph's conclusion was based on a book review by the author sitting next to me.

"I think I know who killed Angela Scott, but the police don't seem to care."

From the article I didn't get the impression the police didn't care. They just didn't have any evidence. What they had was our author's theory... his speculation from a book review. They didn't even have a body, though they did find about four quarts of Angela's blood in a bath tub on Henry Street. They wouldn't have had that if the drain stopper had been pulled out and the shower had been run.

David James' new book, **Shadows of the Empty Necropolis**... *while this book was being written, a woman named Angela Scott was being murdered. James was probably unaware of this, but was Corey Williams who knew Scott from high school?...the trail of Williams to Henry Street...*

I felt like I knew all of the facts in the case, such as they were,

■ ● ■

and that bothered me because I couldn't remember following the story very closely, but they stuck out in my brain almost like it happened yesterday.

I looked up from the article to the author's dull face. His eyes suddenly registered on me. "You'll need money."

I didn't know if it was a hand, or a mouse was climbing up my pant leg. I jumped a little and slid my hand into my pocket where it bumped into a roll of bills. I didn't bother pulling it out to check the denominations. Even if all of the bills were singles and one five, the roll was thick enough to cover my meals and other expenses for a month.

He was staring at me hard. I stared back. "The next time you give me money, just stick it in my hand or put it on the table. Don't try running that 'I used to be a pretty good pickpocket' crap on me. I thought I had a rabid rodent running around in my pant leg."

"Sorry. I used to be a pretty good…"

I put up my hand up to stop him. "Look, the money feels good but I've been up twenty-four hours and I need some sleep. I didn't say I'd take on the job yet."

The author nodded his head up and down. "Another case huh? Let's meet back here tomorrow."

I got up to leave and noticed the waitress wiping down the counter slowly in our direction. Then I wondered what the author was talking about. What case?

I woke up at my place. At least it felt like my place. Seemed a little noisy outside, but that could have been because it was a Friday. I walked across my bedroom and cranked the handle to open the window. I gazed across the boulevard to the building opposite mine. White curtains were waving and shaking from every open window. I wondered how long I had been asleep. I

■●■

absently reached out for my watch on the dresser. It wasn't there, but a framed photo of someone I had never seen before was. It startled me for a second. Goddam Louise! She probably put this photo here as a joke, and she probably even has my watch.

I looked around the room to see if there was any evidence of Louise having been here last night. Maybe something like the remains of a cigarette butt…wait…is Louise still smoking? I shook my head and thought I should get ready to meet the author again.

It felt like a good morning to stroll kind of slowly on my way to the diner and make a stop at the corner newsstand for a paper. Blind Barry Bulova was working the corner.

"B.B.! How you doing this morning?"

"Hey! Mornin', I'm great. The sun's out. I feel good. No one's tried to cheat me with the 'dollar is a five' routine. Yep. Another great day as long as the sun stays out.

I glanced up at an overcast sky that looked like it could pour water straight from the tap at any moment. " Sounds like you're doin' okay B.B."

"That's what I'm saying. It's a beautiful day!"

"B.B., I'm dropping a five here for two papers and a magazine. Keep the change. Take it easy. Gotta run."

"Yer always in a hurry ain't ya? Take it light."

I walked off and B.B. had a big smile on his face while he folded the corners of the bill I left him. A smile crept up on me until I wondered why I did that. Why would I leave a single and announce it was a five. I never did that before. At least I hoped I didn't. Maybe I could straighten it out on my way home. But why would I do that?

Before I pushed through the diner's revolving door, I glanced up at a sketchy sky. Black thunderheads bordered by bright strips of childhood blue. Strange. I shrugged and pushed through the

■ ● ■

door. I sat down at the "L" in the counter. I looked down the counter at the waitress who was under the broken clock with her hands in the till.

"When you get a chance, could I please get a cup of coffee?"

"Hold your horses. I'm countin'."

"When you get a chance, I said. No rush."

"Whyn't you stop botherin' me. You worried I'm not gonna come down there?"

"No. I was worried that you'd ignore me."

"I don't like you so I take my time getting there."

I was staring at her, puzzled by her admission. Even though I was looking right at her, I almost jumped when she slammed the register closed. She walked slowly down her aisle toward me after stopping to pour me a coffee. She put the cup next to my right arm. I was grateful she didn't accidentally pour it on my back while I sat facing the street, leaning against the counter. The shadows of dark clouds and short streams of bright light were running down the street. It reminded me of shadows passing across waist high grass out in the fields on a summer day.

"Hey! Can I have a slice of pie?"

"What kind?"

"Doesn't matter."

"We're out."

"You were out yesterday."

"Might be out tomorrow, too."

"Can I get some scrambled eggs then?"

"Cook ain't here yet."

"Really? Your cook keeps some special hours doesn't she?"

"Not my cook."

I was watching her lean against the counter with her arms crossed. Not a care in the world.

"Why is it that you don't like me?"

■ ● ■

The waitress was examining me like she was surprised I asked. She collected a deep frown, like one she had been saving up just for me. She looked into my eyes with a calm, dismissive scowl. "Because you hurt people." She walked away from me, back toward the register, wiping the counter absently with a rag in her left hand as she went.

I was just about to ask her what she meant when the front door spun and the author walked in. He immediately looked over at the waitress with a Colgate gleam of a smile. She lit up red with her lipstick shining and her eyes twinkling. The author came over and sat down on the next stool. I moved my coffee over in front of me after I turned away from the street. He handed me a manila folder and I waited for him to say something. He kept looking down at the counter.

"Well?"

He peeped at me from the corner of his eye and then looked back down. The waitress put a coffee and a slice of peach pie in front of him. I winced and followed the waitress's walk down her aisle until she leaned against the wall under the broken clock.

"I want you to find the person who killed Angela Scott."

It was an immediate reaction. I could feel sweat breaking out on my back.

"Open the file. That should help."

Again the book review newspaper clipping the author had written. The next sheet was blank. The next sheet had someone's SAT scores and senior year high school grades. The next sheet had a hardware store receipt glued to it. Borax and sponges.

"What the heck is this?! There's nothing here!"

"It's a starting point."

"Starting toward what?!"

"You'll figure it out. That's why I'm paying you."

I sifted through the file again thinking I must have missed

■ ● ■

something. There was nothing to miss.

Are you taking the case?

I looked at the author who was turned to the street, glassy-eyed like he was under some kind of cheap hypnosis. "When will you start?"

When will I start? It felt like a logical question even though it shouldn't have.

I did a double-take like some stranger had slapped me.

"I'll see what I can do." I saw an old friend walk past the diner's windows. "I'll start right now." I jumped up from my stool and pushed my way through the revolving door. I ran up the sidewalk and caught up with my friend, Sam.

"Hey, Sam. How're you doing?"

Sam looked at me and smiled. "Haven't seen you around in a while. You must not be in any trouble. I don't feel any cops around."

"Why would cops be around me?"

Sam's smile grew bigger. "You have trouble around you I only see in my nightmares."

"Are you trying to tell me you don't run with trouble?"

"You know me, I don't mind a reasonable amount of trouble."

"You mean like that kid that's following us?"

"So you picked up on him, too?"

I noticed we were walking up Sutter to Kearney. The kid kept following with his head down.

"I'm going to get some dinner on Powell Street. You want to join me?"

"Nah. I'm going to catch a car. I'm looking for someone."

"Sorry for him. Okay then. Stay out of trouble. You probably don't want to get in as deep as last time." He smiled and saluted.

I ran to the corner to catch a streetcar. When I sat down and looked back, I saw the kid crossing the street in the same direc-

■●■

tion as Sam. What did he mean 'last time'?

I thought I must have been asleep a little. I jumped up and tripped down the streetcar stairs, stumbling over the curb. Where the heck was I? I started to walk to get my bearings. It felt dark and unexpectedly a smile lit up my face. I saw him sitting in a car with headphones on.

"Hey!Lionel!"

His smile was larger than mine. He rolled down the car's window. "Didn't think I'd be seeing you for a long time, crime, wine, shine shinola like shite and I gotta listen billy bop bip.

I don't want to screw up your stakeout. Just want to say 'Hi.' Didn't expect to see you out here."

"I didn't think you'd make bail, out of jail, in the hail, pail, wail, sickly saga story, I still gotta listen." He was tapping me on the shoulder.

He ripped off the headphones, "OH hell gotta go, woe, whoa"…he broke out of the car and charged toward a brownstone. Over his shoulder he yelled, "Don't leave the bodies in the street next time, fine, sign, Coolidge…" He kind of faded out going up the stairs and slamming through the building's doors.

I decided the best thing for me was to keep on walking until I saw something familiar. But I didn't expect it to be someone who was familiar.

He saw me before I saw him.

"Well look who's here. The loogan."

"Hey Phil. How've you been?"

"Pretty jake." He looked around with half a smile on his face. "Where's the bodies?"

"What does that mean?"

"You're kidding me, right?"

He could see I was sore. "You know every time I see you…"

Now he was sore. "Yeah, Yeah. I remind you of Sam."

■ ● ■

"I don't get it. The only thing you two have in common is that you're both tall. You have dark hair and he's almost blond."

"You can cut that out now. I think we know why people get me and Sam confused a little."

"Where you headed for, Phil?"

"I'm going down to that cheap casino to see a guy named Eddie"

"Do I know him?

"Probably not, But he probably would have loved to meet you."

Phil stopped under a tree and adjusted the brim of his fedora." Where are you going? If you're going in my direction maybe I can get you there in my heap."

"I'm headed toward the train station but I think I better walk. I've got some things to work out in my head. But thanks."

"Yeah. Well whatever you end up doing, leave my name out of it."

I nodded like I understood. Phil adjusted his hat again and pulled his raincoat tight. He slid into his Plymouth, lit a cigarette, and was gone. I was standing in the street not having noticed it had rained, watching Phil's taillights fade to black, and wondering what I was doing here.

I started walking, mostly looking at the ground, thinking about Angela Scott and the guy who killed her. Once in a while when the neon light from a bar or restaurant colored the sidewalk, I'd look up.

"Oh, look Asta. We know him don't we? What a surprise. How are you? Here, hold Asta's leash. I'll be right back out. I'll be just second." Taken aback, I watched her walk into the Bakery. The dog pulled on the leash a little trying to follow her.

■ ● ■

A man's deep baritone voice snapped me back to my reality. "What a surprise seeing you here and what are you doing with my dog? Usually I take him on his walks, so Nora must be close by. And, I don't see any cops around so you couldn't have been here long." The whole time he stared at me with his eyelids half closed and a snicker hanging on his lips.

"She's inside the bakery."

"Oh, good. I hope it's a cake. Is it anybody's birthday? And anyways, what are you doing out and about?

"I'm trying to find a murderer."

"One less of those is always a good thing. But avoid mirrors."

"What does that mean?"

He put his open hand on my chest. "Don't get upset, it's just that mirrors can be dangerous things. Sometimes you can see who you are by accident. Here, let me take the leash so you can be on your way. I'll tell Nora you said goodbye."

"I'll tell her myself. Here she comes."

Nick's eyes lit up like the best person in the world was coming through the door.

"Mommy, could you hold that door open a little? I love the aroma of fresh bread."

Nora let go of the door immediately and Nick pretended to pout.

"Before I go…do either of you remember the woman who reported the murder of Angela Scott?"

"I don't, do you Nick?"

Nick gave me a smile with deep dimples. "So that's it. A cold case, huh? You know, there's a woman who would probably know down on… oh, where is it, don't remember. Sorry."

"Nick, I think I need a drink."

"I will definitely join you. Want to join us? You'll have to promise not to shoot anyone on the way."

■ ● ■

"Nah. I better get going. For some reason I feel like I'm running out of time."

"Okay, then." Nick tipped his hat and the two of them sauntered off with the dog tugging on her leash leading the way.

I started walking again ignoring the light from bars or bakeries that occasionally lit up the sidewalk. Unconsciously I ended up across from the train station. A small flood of people were coming out. I started to cross the street and I yelled, "Ray! Raymond!"

Raymond looked at me and slid a hand inside his jacket. He looked impeccable all the way down to his spats. His smile glittered with gold, but it wasn't a real smile. It was more like, 'I know who you are and I ain't afraid of you' (Just lettin' you know.)

"How you been Ray? And how's Eze?

"We be doin' fine."

Raymond was the most dangerous man I knew. It felt like he was giving me some kind of respect I didn't understand. His hand was still inside his jacket.

"You come for me?"

I was taken aback. More like stunned. What did he mean? I fought through my confusion and said, "No. I'm trying to track someone down who killed a woman named Angela Scott"

Ray was looking at me with one of the strangest gazes I had ever seen. It was like he was looking down from space and could see everything that was happening but didn't understand a thing. His hand slid out of his jacket and he buttoned up his purple double-breasted blazer.

"He a dead man then, ain't he." He said it like it was a foregone conclusion. I didn't know what to say.

"Ray, there's an overweight woman who runs with a little guy named Donald. You know who I'm talking about?" Raymond

■ ● ■

nodded. "You seen them around?"

Raymond looked at me with a money sign on his face. I pulled out the roll the author had given me and peeled off two bills with the kite flyer on them. Ray's eyes lit up.

"Bertha and the little guy is Donald. Think he used to be a lawyer. Gimme something to write with. I gave him a pen that always leaked and my newspaper. I handed over the two bills and Raymond gave me back the newspaper...with a serious scowl.

"Get a new pen. Look at my fingers. Now I gotta go back in there and clean up."

"Sorry, Ray." He shrugged and shook his head like he was asking me, 'What's wrong with you'?

"Okay then. I'ma meet a couple of people." Ray started to put his hand up to the brim of his homburg. Suddenly he stopped and he switched to his clean hand and straightened his hat. I watched him disappear back into Union Station and then I set off for the address Ray had given me.

I took an elevator up to the office. I said "Hi!" to the secretary. "Is your boss in?" "Bertha is here. Donald is out."

I walked into Bertha's office unannounced. "Who the hell do you think you are?!" Money means nothing to you!" Bertha's back was to me until she swiveled around in her chair. It looked like all the color in her face escaped. Her grey eyes went flat.

"Sorry. I thought you were my partner." Her eyes were all over me. What the heck was she looking for?

"And here I am." Donald walked in silently behind me.

"Sometimes I feel like I could rip your heart out by the roots."

"We need to give Elsie a raise."

"What?!"

"You basically have her doing two jobs."

"My head shifted from one to the other. I noticed the col-

■ ● ■

or came back to Bertha's cheeks and her eyes had a twinkle in them.

Donald looked at me sullenly, ignoring the argument he had been in. "Are you here to see me or Bertha?"

"I need to find someone who knew a woman named Angela Scott."

Behind me I could hear Bertha sigh in relief.

"Let's take a walk."

Donald lit a cigarette and I followed him out to the street.

"What's the idea of scaring Bertha like that?"

"All I did was walk in."

"You should know that's enough."

I wanted to ask why, but I held my tongue.

"About Angela Scott then."

"There's a woman who lives on Henry Street that used to know her. But don't make it messy, okay? We don't need the cops around here for days scaring off trade like that last time."

I stared at him and he gave me a wry smile back. "This woman sits in a café at the corner of Henry most evenings."

I walked over to the café at Henry Street and Hopper that looked like it could have been anywhere.

A woman was sitting at a table next to the windows. There was a guy behind the horseshoe counter serving coffee to a man and a woman at the far side of the counter.

When the woman at the window saw me, she jumped up immediately. I ran to the door to cut her off when she came out.

"Hey! Slow down. I want to talk to you." She looked terrified. "I just want to talk, okay?"

"About what?"

I want to talk to you about your old friend Angela Scott." Her shoulders dropped. "Okay. Let's go to my place."

"We could talk right here in the café."

■●■

"I don't want to cause a problem for them inside. And you'll be more comfortable at my place."

I don't know why she thought I'd be more comfortable at her place. She had a two room apartment with an old wooden table in the kitchen area with two rickety wooden chairs under a bare light bulb hanging over the table. There was a bakelite radio on a shelf over the sink with the cord held together with tape. The front was cracked under the dial.

"You were a friend of Angela Scott?"

"Kind of."

"What's that mean? Were you a friend of hers or not?"

I looked at her while trying not to fall over with the chair.

"How well did you know her?"

"Pretty much intimately."

"Did you see her the night she was murdered?

"Kind of."

"Look! Help me out. I'm trying to find the guy who killed her and I have the impression that you can help me."

Suddenly she had tears in her eyes.

"I don't think you need to find anyone"

"Why do you say that?"

"Because I'm Angela Scott and you're here to kill me."

She was crying now. I reached inside my jacket for a handkerchief. What the hell?! There was a gun wrapped in the handkerchief. What the hell was going on here?!!

Did the author who 'used to be a very good pickpocket' put it there? You can't be Angela. The Police even know she was murdered."

We sat glancing at each other furtively for about ten minutes. This all made no sense and it made perfect sense. I stood up and unwrapped the gun. I handed Angela the handkerchief.

"Time to break the rules."

■ ● ■

"What?"

Now what? She had stopped crying and rolled the cloth into a ball and handed it back to me. I started to put the ball over the muzzle. I couldn't stifle my laughter. What the hell good would that do? I jammed the kerchief into my pocket.

We were so close it was hard to miss her. When I was starting to walk out the door, I paused to touch the two bullet holes in the wall. Angela was crying again. "Disappear okay? And good luck."

"My luck is only as good as your luck."

Whatever the hell that meant. Angela gave me the feeling she knew what was going on more than I did. Maybe it was supposed to be like that, but right now there were no questions I wanted to ask because I was going home. Right now. I almost ran down the stairs from her apartment out into the air that felt like freedom.

I caught a trolley that seemed to come out of nowhere, no questions. I was riding and glad of it. I walked up the stairs to my apartment slowly. Now there were questions but they would all have to be answered tomorrow. When I walked into my bedroom I could hear heavy breathing. The half light from the street let me see a woman's face I didn't recognize. I stepped back nervously and studied her face. Then I looked at the photo on my dresser. I felt nauseous. It was the woman in my bed.
I whispered "Louise?"

She rolled over. "Wha?…come to bed."

I pulled off my pants, got under the covers and let a woman named Louise put her arm over my shoulder while I cried silently into the semi-dark.

Louise was gone when I woke up. It seemed quieter than yesterday. I walked to the diner and on the way stopped for a paper. Blind Billy carried on about the weather. I took the roll of

■●■

bills out of my pocket and dropped two Ulysses in his cup. I felt better about myself, but I was still anxious. I walked up to the diner counter where the waitress had her hands in the till.

"Don't bother me, I'm countin.'"

I leaned over the counter and peered into the register tray.

"There's nothing in there. What are you counting?"

"Go sit your ass down! I'm counting whatever is in here!"

She slammed the register closed so hard, I jumped.

"What the hell do you want, nosey?"

"A coffee would be fine."

The Waitress's face lit up. I turned to see the author push through the revolving door.

He sat down by the L in the counter. I joined him. She put down two cups of coffee.

"And here's a slice of Strawberry Rhubarb pie."

"Can I get one of those?"

"Sorry… that was the last slice." She walked away humming.

"How're you doing on the search for the murderer?"

"Pretty good… There is no murderer."

"What the hell are you talking about?!"

"I talked to Angela Scott last night."

"No you didn't.'

"I did and you probably know that I did. You understand the whole thing…"

"And now you do too?"

"Pretty much. Are you hoping to eliminate enough characters that all this will end? Is that why you hired me?"

He suddenly had one tear rolling over his left cheek.

"I can't live like this!

"Why not? Of course you can. That woman down there under that broken clock is absolutely in love with you for as long this lasts."

■ ● ■

"What if it ends tomorrow?"

"Isn't that what you were trying for anyway? So you'll just be in love forever."

"What will you do?"

"I'm going to try to figure something out.

"You mean a way out?"

"Maybe…maybe for all of us. Maybe with some inspiration.

The author stared at me like he was in terror. I looked back with a smile on my face.

"She'll always love you. Go over there and make you and her happy."

I turned away from him and watched paper dance on the wind past the windows and...

■ ● ■

THE END

■ ● ■

About the Author

L ee Brown is a former trade union organizer. Before moving
to New York City from Binghamton, N.Y., he was the found-
ing president of Local 994 of the International Chemical Workers
Union. In NYC he worked with the ILGWU, organizing shops in
New York's garment center and in Brooklyn. As a community organizer he was active in housing issues and in the anti-apartheid
movement. Before taking up writing fiction, Lee led a rock band
called "Patterns of Grace," and he owned a coffeehouse for fifteen
years. If he were forced to pick three favorite current writers,
they would be Mosley, Miéville and Modiano. He loves watching
the NBA and Canadian football. Lee has two wonderful daughters
(whom he shares with his best friend and former wife, Amy
Manso) and two grandsons, who he hopes, in the future, will con-
tinue the struggle for the rights of workers everywhere.

Lee is a member of the Crime Writers of Color.

■ ● ■

www.ingramcontent.com/pod-product-compliance
Lightning Source LLC
Chambersburg PA
CBHW030132260626
47156CB00008B/2914